House on the Harbor

a birch harbor novel

ELIZABETH BROMKE

Cover design by Red Leaf Book Design

HOUSE ON THE HARBOR
Published by:
Elizabeth Bromke
White Mountains, Arizona

For my sisters, Kara and Erin.

Chapter 1—Kate

A light breeze curled in from the window. On it, the scent of lavender. Faint but sweet.

In front of each window in her suburban Michigan home, Kate Hannigan had strategically positioned fragrant plants of many varieties.

When the weather was just right, Kate would throw open the windows and revel in the aroma like a newly appointed florist.

It was a trick her mother had taught her four daughters. *Why use candles when you have flowers and a breeze?* Nora Hannigan had often chided her daughters.

Kate happened to love candles as much as she loved taking in the earthy smell of Mother Nature. But still. It was a good thought. A good reminder of her mother. A happy one.

She smiled to herself, swept up the last pot—the one at her bedside window—and carried it downstairs, where her sisters waited.

"Last one?" Megan asked, tugging at a stiff, black pencil skirt.

"Last one," Kate replied, handing the lavender to her.

Megan transferred the purple-budded flower to a long, narrow folding table that stretched in front of the sitting room window.

Every single one of Kate's little potted plants was now resituated tastefully for the reception. Kate was good at that sort of thing. Adding the perfect touch to a space. Bringing it *to life*.

And yet, together, in the front room, all of that lavender and jasmine and gardenia achieved more of a funeral parlor effect than that of a florist shop. Though appropriate, it didn't sit well with Kate. For, this event was meant to be less *funereal* and more *floral*. Even if it *was* a funeral.

She frowned.

Clara stole a cube of cheese and popped it into her mouth. “I'm starving,” the youngest Hannigan sister mumbled through a mouthful.

Kate snapped her fingers. “I know.” She strode to the window, unlatched the levers, and slid it wide open.

The cool morning breeze lifted her blonde, shoulder-length tresses up off her neck and blew in some much-needed fresh air.

“Good call,” Amelia said. “It was feeling a little... ”

“A little *funeral-y*?” Megan read Kate's mind. Of the four sisters, Kate and Megan resembled each other the least, in part because Megan insisted on dying her hair to match her wardrobe: black. But they shared one important commonality: a critical nature. It was a trait passed down from Nora, no doubt.

Amelia, the second oldest, was something of a silly heart, even as she ascended in age. The lighthearted nature was a characteristic that originated with their father and one that only Amelia had been gifted.

Kate was more like Megan (and Nora), discerning—though less morbid and more grounded.

Clara was neither silly nor critical. She fell somewhere in between. Anxious and, well, young.

Presently, Clara grinned at Megan's morbid joke. Then Amelia chuckled. Soon enough all four of them were laughing together. And then, crying.

Again.

"Will we *ever* get over this?" Clara asked, pushing her thumbs along her lower lash line to clear away remnants of the spontaneous sob session.

Kate smiled at her and pulled her in for a hug. "No, we won't," she replied, locking eyes with Amelia, whose smooth pale face was scrunching again into a fresh round of tears. "But," Kate went on, "that doesn't mean we'll never laugh again. Or be happy again."

Clara nodded into Kate's shoulder and lifted her head. "I'm fine," she said. "*We're* fine."

"True," Megan replied, tugging Clara onto the love seat with her and leaning back into the pillowy cushions. "We're fine. It was her time. Oh, boy, was it her time, you know?"

Kate eyed Megan.

After a brief sigh, Megan brushed a black strand of hair out of her eyes and offered an explanation. "She was going downhill. Deteriorating, even." She stopped and smiled, a sentimental, weepy smile, her green eyes turning glassy. "For all we know, the poor thing was driving herself mad. I'd imagine the disease does that, right? Anyway, I don't think Nora would have wanted to be what she was becoming."

Megan had called their mother by her first name since Megan was a teenager, and Nora had long given up the fight against it. It no longer felt disrespectful, in fact. Just one of those quirks a family had.

Regardless of the name matter, Megan was right.

It was their mom's *time.*

And it was also time for the reception to begin. Kate and her sisters had left the burial ahead of everyone by a mere ten minutes. All they had to do when they got to her house was set up the food and flowers. Relatives had agreed to handle everything else.

Kate wasn't sold on the paper products and plastic utensils, but the others overruled her, arguing that the last thing they needed after Mom's funeral was to do dishes.

Kate would argue that dishes would be the exact sort of thing she'd need.

Cleaning, to Kate, was therapy.

She checked her wristwatch, a thin leather strap with a silver face. "They'll be here soon," she announced and glanced around the room, anxious.

On the folding table, now framed perfectly by two sentinel lavender plants, sat orderly trays of cold cuts and cheese, a platter of fruits and vegetables, and a bald spot at the far end dedicated for everything else due to arrive with their aunts and cousins.

Amelia fussed with the memorial setting, which she had first established on a second square folding table, only to move it to the coffee table, and then finally to the back of the upright piano that took up the far corner of the room. "Does this work?" she wondered aloud.

Kate joined her and tweaked the centerpiece—a glass frame, behind which preened their mother in a formal portrait.

No husband sat next to Nora.

No daughters crowded in behind Nora.

Just Nora.

And that sort of photograph was perfect, because it was *Nora's* day, Kate had reminded her sisters.

Not theirs.

Only Amelia had argued, but now she seemed pleased enough. "I remember when Mom had that photo taken," she murmured.

Kate felt her throat close up a bit but swallowed it down.

The crying was supposed to end with the funeral. She promised herself that, as hostess and eldest daughter, it was her duty to see to the perfect reception. A light, happy affair.

In fact, it would be the last event she would have in her home. Because soon she'd be moving. Though to where, exactly, was still unclear.

"I'm not trying to gossip, but did any of you see Matt Fiorillo's date at the service last night?" Amelia asked, pushing a strand of her long brown hair back into position behind her ear as she went for a cheese cube, too.

Matt Fiorillo was, if recent reports were accurate, a local property investor. Also, an old family friend. An old flame, too. One who Kate hoped would stay squarely in her past. But there he was, at the funeral. Typical.

Megan chimed in next. "She might be a prostitute."

Kate shook her head and glared. "Enough, you two," she threatened through a tight voice, then pressed her fingers to her shoulders, ensuring her bra straps were in position squarely beneath the black fabric of her chiffon dress.

Kate hated chiffon.

But her mother had loved it.

It was important to make sacrifices for family. Even chiffon-loving ones. Even dead ones, too.

Kate shook the thought just as the doorbell rang.

"They're here," Amelia announced, her face morphing into a Picasso painting, yet again.

"Keep it together," Kate hissed, holding up her palm. "We can do this." She nodded at the three women, each of whom was on the brink of hysterics.

Kate willed herself to stay sane in the face of grief.

Smoothing her dress and taking in a deep, calming breath, she answered the door.

***

In poured a steady stream of well-wishers, many of whom had attended the wake the evening prior, some who'd also shown up for the burial that morning.

Both the wake and the burial had been formal affairs, drawing oversized attention from Birch Harbor locals. The usual suspects, really. Those of the Actons—their father's side—who were still alive and then Nora's own strained relations.

The strain had begun years back, when Nora refused to take (or give) her husband's last name. Apparently when she'd married, the Hannigans and relatives hoped to shake her loose and prevent the black sheep that Nora was from soiling a good family name.

They were unsuccessful.

In addition to the Actons and Hannigans, Megan's daughter and Kate's sons were also there. Grandchildren were better capable of handling funerals. They were young and distracted. Full of hope. Far separated from the reaching hands of death, to be sure. They'd been catching up together in the backyard, like old times, and Kate had left them to do just that.

Nora was survived by her country club cronies and church friends, too. And other, more anonymous men and women, clad in dutiful black, their expressions appropriately ashen, arrived for the service and would leave after tight goodbyes with Kate and her sisters.

Even Birch Harbor's mayor made a somber (if opportunistic) appearance, bringing with her several members of the town council, the same town council their mother had frequently come to blows with over any number of local dramas.

Others showed up, as well. Local business owners and shopkeepers, like Matt Fiorillo's extended family. And, Nora's lawyer, Michael Matuszewski and entourage.

They drove in a slow convoy all the way to Kate's house out on Apple Tree Hill. It was a solid forty-five-minute drive inland, away from the harbor and closer to Detroit.

Kate was impressed.

She ushered them in politely, accepting rehearsed lines at the front door while Megan lingered behind her, ready to help if Kate faltered.

Megan was a good sister that way. Austere, sure. But stable. Helpful.

Clara had disappeared into the kitchen as soon as the first group arrived, no doubt hiding. Clara was something of a hider. Kate chalked that up to her relative immaturity. She was sixteen years younger than Kate, after all, and only now in her twenties.

Kate watched in amusement as Amelia, predictably, played the receiving widow. Or widower. Or... orphan? Whatever her label, the chestnut-haired actress shined in the role, greeting each visitor with grace and gratitude, blinking away tears at the very mention of their mom. The tears were surely genuine, but Amelia's earnest nods at every memory each of the near-strangers tried to evoke was an act. She was a good person to have on hand.

The reception began easily, with extended family taking on the role of hosting, more or less.

"Matt's here." Clara had reappeared at Kate's side, her attention now entirely fixed on any opportunity for distraction. All four sisters stood together on the threshold between the foyer and the parlor. It was the perfect people-watching position.

"Are you going to talk to him?" Amelia asked.

Kate shook her head and narrowed her eyes. "I haven't talked to him in years. Now's not the time for a reunion." The sisters gazed together across the room. Kate gestured discreetly with her drink. "There he is. By Mom's picture."

"Why is he wearing a turtleneck in May?" Clara asked.

"I like turtlenecks," Megan replied, taking up for him.

Kate scoffed. "He never had good fashion sense."

"It's not the turtleneck," Clara whispered conspiratorially.

The three others leaned in closer.

Clara went on. "It's the *woman*."

Kate bit the insides of her cheeks and caught Amelia nodding gravely. "Yes, I saw her, too."

Finally, Kate broke. "Where?" She lowered her plastic cup of lemonade and scanned the room.

Amelia lifted an eyebrow and thrust her chin to the far corner, just behind where Matt stood.

Kate took in the woman, and she was surprised to see her sisters' estimations proved valid. Clad in a black spaghetti-string top, black jeans, and black flip-flops, the poor thing was decidedly out of place.

"I suppose a black outfit isn't enough to fit in at a funeral," Megan mused behind them, her voice appropriately lifeless.

Kate narrowed her eyes on the woman, a realization hitting her. "That's not even a *woman*," she hissed, turning away and facing her sisters out of mortification. "It's a *teenager*."

"Teenager?" Clara craned her neck around Kate. "Oh my word, you're right. She must be in eighth or ninth grade!" Clara, Megan, and Amelia's eyes grew wide.

"Sh, *sh!* It's not his *girlfriend*. It's got to be his *daughter*."

Again, Kate's three sisters looked past her with sharp affects.

Finally, Clara relaxed back into position and sipped her lemonade. "You're right. That girl is no older than fourteen. Maybe even thirteen now that I'm looking. She must go to St. Mary's. I've never seen her at school."

"What is he even doing here?" Amelia asked, breathing deeply, for Kate's benefit, probably.

Megan shook her head. "Everyone wants a piece of the pie."

At that, Kate snorted. "Come on. As *if*. Matt doesn't care about money, anyway. At least, he didn't when *I* knew him."

"Maybe Matt has a heart of gold. But look around you, Kate." Megan lifted her plastic cup in appraisal of the packed room. "As far as the locals know, Nora Hannigan was the Queen of Birch Harbor, a glittery benefactor, primed to dole out her estate to anyone who so much as waved at her. As far as they know, Mom was rich. And generous, too."

Kate swallowed Megan's words, her eyes lingering on Matt. Down deep inside, she wanted to go to him. She wanted to ask why he showed up. Who his little girl was. Where he'd been.

But she knew. He'd been right there. In Birch Harbor. Matt, unlike Kate, wasn't one to run from the past.

Chapter 2—Amelia

One week later.

Amelia-Ann Hannigan stood in front of her foggy bathroom mirror and patted her face dry. Raw skin glowed back at her. It had taken far too long to scrub away every last bit of rouge and kohl she'd painstakingly applied for the wrap party the night before.

No, she wasn't the star of the show. Or even a supporting player. But Amelia considered herself to be a professional. And despite her pitifully tiny role as an extra in Little City Theatre's production of *Oklahoma!* she wanted to prove to her director that she had potential. Even at the ripe old age of forty-something. Hah.

Anyway, the makeup helped to conceal the bags beneath her eyes from traveling to and from Birch Harbor for her mother's funeral.

Still, it shouldn't take nearly half an hour of washcloth-rubbing to get rid of her "face."

Quietly, she promised herself to scale back a little on the makeup, even for rehearsals and performances and wrap parties. Amelia really wasn't old enough to "put on her face" for any event.

Maybe she should lose five or ten pounds. Then, the struggling actress wouldn't have to obsess over adding hollows to her cheeks with shadowy browns and angles to her cheekbones with shimmery highlighter crayons.

Amelia was too young for a full face but too old for trying to look twenty.

It was a hard spot to be in. Part of her wished to age enough to nab those "north-of-fifty" roles, part of her contemplated premature plastic surgery to better achieve the fresh-out-of-college-cover-girl roles.

Fat chance.

Amelia was due back in Birch Harbor that evening. Instead of flying this time, she planned to drive. Jimmy, her boyfriend of six months, was supposed to stay at her apartment and watch after Dobi, Amelia's paunchy Weiner dog.

She'd half-heartedly considered bringing both of them. Ever since the funeral, Amelia could not shake the longing in the pit of her stomach.

Loneliness.

The realization that Amelia was entering middle age with little to show for it. No husband. No children (save for Dobi). No mortgage.

And now, no mother.

Losing her mom was hard as hell. Really, it was.

Plus, the whole thing was made harder by Amelia's stark realization that she was bound on the same journey as sweet-and-spicy Nora, a wacky spinster whose closest friends were more often her most poisonous enemies.

And that just wasn't Amelia-Ann Hannigan. She was not a wacky spinster. Even more than that, she had friends. *Real* ones, who weren't *also* her enemies—that was important to note, a big difference between Amelia and her mother. Nora may have put on a show for the public, but her actress-daughter was the real deal. A good friend. Not a fake.

So, maybe no husband, children, mortgage, or mother... but Amelia *did* have friends. And a boyfriend, hapless though he may be. And a furbaby. And sisters.

And, hopefully—if her recent on-Broadway meet-and-greet was well-received, she might just have an exciting gig, to boot.

"Making it" in New York had been even harder than she thought it would be. Twenty years of working her way toward The Big Apple, one small-town community theatre at a time, had resulted in a demotion, actually.

Bit parts in off-Broadway productions that were poorly attended. So poorly attended, that she had to make ends meet elsewhere.

Waiting tables sucked. Plain and simple.

Who wanted to be a forty-year-old waitress? Much less, an over-forty waitress who was trying desperately to break into the ingénue-favoring theatre world?

Well, maybe *some* people. But not *Amelia-Ann.*

Now, as she felt herself pulled right and left by what she did not have and what she *did* have, she tucked away every last jar, tube, can, and palette of her makeup set and kept out *only* her mascara.

Three swipes. That's all she allowed herself. Three quick swipes before popping the brush back in its tube and the tube in her bag and zipping it with finality.

Less is more, Amelia-Ann, the voice in her head trilled.

"When you going?"

It was Jimmy, leaning shirtless in the doorway.

He had absolutely no reason to be shirtless. He'd just arrived minutes earlier—fully clothed. Amelia had given him zero reason to undress. And there he was, an almost-six pack bulging beneath his shaved chest. Completely unnecessary.

But that was Jimmy.

"Now," she answered, pecking him on the cheek before squeezing past to hunt down Dobi for a goodbye cuddle.

"I've always wanted to go to Michigan, you know." Jimmy crossed his arms over his chest, flexing his pecs involuntarily.

That pang—that longing from the week before grew heavy in her stomach.

Her sisters would hate Jimmy. Amelia was sure of that. And Clara's tiny little apartment had no room for a fledgling couple. It would be weird to invite him. If Amelia didn't realize this before, she did now.

She bit down on her lip and raised her eyebrows at her brooding, out-of-work, *younger* boyfriend.

She sighed. "Jimmy, I would love for you to come... " she started, suddenly feeling torn all over again.

"You would?" he asked, the corners of his mouth curling up in a lazy grin.

"Well, of course," she replied, scooping Dobi into her arms and scratching beneath his collar. "But Clara only has a fold-out sofa."

"I bet we can fit," he answered, his voice dropping an octave as he uncrossed his arms and strode to her.

Amelia closed her eyes, her heart racing in her chest. She opened her eyes and lifted one palm against him. "I'm so sorry. Clara is super prim and proper. It's a no. It's such a no, and I'm *so* sad about it." She put on a pout. Dobi let out a low growl.

He took a step back and raised his hands in surrender. "All right. I get it."

"Oh, Jimmy, honey," Amelia set Dobi on the overstuffed armchair and reached for her roll-on suitcase. "I *want* you to come. But you'd be bored. I'll be with the probate attorney and my *sisters*, and—"

"I get it," he answered, letting her hug his torso as he gazed off.

"I've got an idea!" Amelia's eyes flashed open. The perfect solution occurred to her. A light at the end of the tunnel. A way for her to quell the pit in her stomach with a little hope. "Why don't you come down this *weekend*? We can play tourist for my last day in Birch Harbor. You could rent a car and drive to the lake. That way you don't have to be around for the lawyer stuff, but you can still meet my sisters, maybe, and see my hometown. We'll ride back to the city together. A mini-vacay. What do you think?"

He smirked. "Yeah, maybe."

Amelia smiled and threw one more look at Dobi, the one she really wanted to take. But she knew this was for the best. Her attention could be on all the legal stuff that would no doubt be confusing and stressful.

Then, when it was over—she'd enjoy the reward of reuniting with Dobi and put on her docent hat for Jimmy. Maybe, just maybe, seeing him outside the city would do her good, anyway. Give her some perspective. An answer. Maybe it would show her whether he was commitment-worthy or just another unemployed construction worker looking for love. Or, lust.

Maybe Jimmy could even help, in some way.

Her boyfriend was a bit of a project, but Amelia was not afraid of a project.

She bid them both goodbye and trotted down four flights of stairs and out onto the busy thoroughfare.

She took a cab to the car rental place and accepted their cheapest offering: a smoky, puke-smelling sedan that, with any luck, would take her directly to the car rental hub nearest Birch Harbor where she could deposit it and be whisked away by Clara, who, naturally, drove a cute little VW Bug. One that didn't smell like an ashtray or a vomit bag.

***

"Amelia!"

Amelia whipped around just as she passed the single key over the counter to the car rental guy. It was Clara, waving wildly from the curb.

She smiled and waved back, thanking the clerk and wheeling her luggage through the greasy doors and out into the warm Michigan afternoon.

Clara rounded her car and squeezed Amelia in a tight hug. "I'm so glad you're here," she gushed.

Amelia hugged back, hard. "*I'm* so glad I'm here. I forget that New York sort of has a smell to it. Until I leave."

"You mean to tell me that place doesn't have a smell to it?" Clara pointed behind her toward the boxy, dated building that was once a fast-food joint.

"Touché," Amelia replied. "But out here? It's... *nice*." She hugged Clara again, and they drove together back into Birch Harbor.

"How was your week?" Clara asked, adjusting her grip on the steering wheel.

"Busy. We wrapped *Oklahoma!* I packed to come back. Dobi is with Jimmy. I should have just brought him."

"Jimmy or Dobi?"

"Dobi," Amelia replied pointedly.

Clara grinned. "How's that going, anyway?"

"You mean with Jimmy?"

"Yeah. Isn't he... *younger*?" Clara lifted an eyebrow at her older sister.

Amelia blew out a sigh and tugged her ponytail loose, letting her warm chestnut waves fall around her shoulders. "Jimmy is... a good guy."

"When did you two start dating again?" Clara's voice was light, but her words were heavy.

"Um, December? It was right after we got Mom's diagnosis."

"Oh, yeah." Clara brought a second hand to the steering wheel and switched lanes after checking over her shoulder.

"How'd you meet?"

Amelia frowned. Clara wasn't the type to put twenty questions to her older sisters. "At a bar. I was... I was there with Mia. Actually, it was the exact day I found out. I remember now. I drove here the next morning. But the night before, well. I was a wreck. Mia tried to distract me. And, we met Jimmy. He got my number."

Clara didn't respond, instead maneuvering off the highway and down toward the water.

Birch Harbor. A tourist community on Lake Huron known for its small-town feel, ocean-like beaches, and quaint lakeside eateries.

Just before they pulled up to Clara's digs, The Bungalows—a group of four ground-level units, owned by the Hannigan family trust—Amelia's phone buzzed with a new text.

She opened it up and saw two faces looking back at her: Jimmy and Dobi, posing in front of the very same car rental agency where she'd been just hours before. Jimmy stood there, grinning from ear to ear, dangling a single key above little Dobi's worried face.

A caption below the attached image read: *The tourists are on their way!*

Chapter 3—Clara

"It's tiny. I'm sorry." Clara winced at Amelia as she opened the door to her one-bedroom apartment. "If you decide you want to stay out of town at Kate's or even Megan's… "

Clara watched her sister's expression closely, looking for signs of disgust or, worse, disinterest.

Amelia walked around like she was shopping for houses, inspecting the insides of drawers and touching the curtains, testing their heft. "I love this place. You know that," she cooed at last. "But… "

Clara frowned. "But?"

"I just got a text from Jimmy. He's on his *way*."

"On his way? *Here*?"

Now it was Amelia's turn to cringe. "Yep." She strolled back to where Clara stood in the center of the modest living space, just feet away from the breakfast bar—the only eating area the little bungalow offered. "I'll get a hotel room. I know Kate and Megan would never invite him either." She laughed lightly before adding, "Don't worry."

But it wasn't Jimmy that bothered Clara. In fact, Clara was excited to meet Jimmy. He was super attractive (from the photos she'd seen) and the way Amelia described him, he sounded *fun*.

He was not what bothered her.

It was that Amelia was happy to make different plans. After all that scrubbing and bleaching and sheet-changing and… *prepping*, she was going to stay somewhere else. Clara's face fell.

"I'm so sorry, Clara. I did *not* invite him. I promise."

"Why doesn't he stay here, too?" Clara suggested, crossing her arms over her tunic. "You can sleep in my room with me. He can have the sofa."

"I'd hate to impose him on you like that," Amelia whined. "Ugh. I'm just, I don't know, *trapped* with this guy. I mean, I like Jimmy. I really do, but... "

"It's completely fine by me. You can share my bed, unless you two... " Clara raised her eyebrows to her sister. She felt her neck grow warm at the thought of housing a total stranger. It nearly ruined the day. Clara could just imagine cleaning the toilet after a sloppy New York construction worker type. And what did he sleep in? Boxers? She shuddered involuntarily.

"You know what? I didn't *invite* Jimmy. Neither did you. He can get a room at the motel." Amelia smirked. "What about Dobi though?"

"Pets welcome! Dobi can stay here, of course," Clara answered, feeling her excitement return. "There's a courtyard out back. I think another resident has a little Chihuahua, in fact."

"Okay." Amelia let out a breath and clapped her hands together. "Let's do it. I'll tell Jimmy to book a room because I promised I was staying *with you*, which is true. And your place is too small for him, which is also true."

Clara nodded vigorously. "Yes, it'll be great."

"It's settled, then," Amelia added with a mock-serious expression.

Clara beamed up at her older sister. "Wonderful. All right, back to the tour?"

"Yes." Amelia smiled. "Back to the tour."

***

After showing Amelia her bedroom and bathroom, the tiny kitchen, and then how to pull out the sofa into a bed, they went over an itinerary Clara had put together.

"We meet with the attorney tomorrow at eight. Kate said to expect to be there for two hours, max. It will be the first meeting, and there could be several more," Clara explained.

Amelia nodded along as she sipped from a can of Diet Coke at the breakfast bar. "Kate said we might be able to get a few meetings set up over the course of this week. That way I don't have to drive back and forth. That's why I'm staying through Saturday. I'll find out this week if I got *Lady Macbeth*. I had a pseudo audition, you see. If I do—fingers crossed—then rehearsals will *probably* start next Monday." She grinned excitedly.

Clara squealed for Amelia. "*Macbeth*? That's like, *huge*, Amelia."

Amelia nodded and bit down on her lower lip. "I know. We'll see." Her face fell a little. "Regardless, Mario only gave me this week off from The Bread Basket. He won't hold my job after Saturday. Or so he *says*. Anyway, I'm hoping we settle everything *now*."

Clara shrugged. "Maybe. But that only works if the attorney can meet after three. I mean, at least, for *me*. I have to work every day, remember? My principal got a sub for tomorrow morning, but beyond that I risk going over my paid leave. If we can push any future meetings to June, that'd be really great. I'll be out of school by then, you know. But I think Kate is hoping to settle it sooner."

"We could probably have video calls, worst case scenario. And if something needs to be signed—well, it's the twenty-first century. The internet, you know."

Taking a sip of her own Diet Coke, Clara blinked. "Yeah. That's true. I just... I just want it to be all done, too. You know?"

Her older sister smiled and draped her arm across Clara's shoulders. "Me, too. We'll do whatever we can. And besides, Kate says Mom had everything in place. There shouldn't be any surprises. Equal division, then we go our separate ways. Full freedom to follow our dreams."

An itchy feeling crept up Clara's spine. She already *was* following her dream. What her sister had said felt tacky. Morbid. Tasteless, even. She pushed away her soda can and pulled out her phone to pretend to check for messages. "Yeah. It'll be fine," she muttered petulantly. Clara never had been good at confronting her older sisters.

She felt Amelia study her. "So, do you like teaching?"

Putting the phone to sleep, Clara blinked and met her sister's gaze. "I love it. Love the kids. Love summer vacation. It's really great." An involuntary smile lifted her cheeks. Her back stopped itching. She waited for another question about her career.

But Amelia lifted her chin and changed the line of questioning. "Are you dating?"

Clara shook her head, flushing. "No." She pulled the soda can back and took a small sip, but Amelia was still watching her, an eyebrow poised high on her forehead, willing her little sister to go on.

Clara took the hint and shook her head again. "It's *Birch Harbor*, Amelia. No one here is single. And if they are single, then they're tourists. Dating doesn't exist in Birch Harbor. Not for me, at least."

It was true. Clara had gone out a couple of times, thanks to her friends making a profile for her on a dating app. But each date had been with a guy who lived in or near Detroit. It was painfully awkward when she had to ask that they meet halfway between. Nothing had ever materialized. Which was fine by Clara. She had her career. And, up until recently, she had her mother to care for. Lingering sadness crawled up her throat and threatened to spill out, but she stalled it, swallowing hard.

"I didn't believe in marriage, you know," Amelia said quietly.

"What?" Clara was confused. Amelia never let a week go by without securing a boyfriend for herself—or nurturing a useless relationship. "You love men."

Amelia broke into a cackle. "I 'love men'? What does *that* mean?"

Clara blushed. "I mean, you always have a boyfriend. And when you don't, you're looking for one."

"Like I said, I *used* to not believe. I think that's changing now. With Mom, and... age, I guess. I spent many years thinking commitment could look different."

"It *can* look different. Marriage isn't the only way to commit." As the words formed on her tongue, Clara knew they'd bounce out as disingenuously as they felt. For Clara, it would be marriage or bust. She was no floozy.

But Amelia shook her head. "I don't buy that anymore, Clara. I don't know. Maybe I'm getting a little more... " She searched for the right word, but Clara knew where she was going.

"A little more like *me*?"

This time, they shared the laugh. "Yes. A little more traditional. Like my millennial kid sister, ironically."

"I want to be married one day, that's true. But I'm not in a rush. I've got my job. And my sisters." Clara knew she sounded lame, but she didn't care. It was the truth. The furthest thing from her mind was dating around. "Do you think you'll marry Jimmy?"

Amelia made a face. "No."

"Then why are you staying with him?" Clara asked. An honest question.

After a beat, her sister took another sip and stood up. "Maybe I will, I guess. If things change, maybe I will."

Clara left the conversation alone and joined Amelia in a little stretch.

"So what's next?" the older one asked.

"According to my itinerary, we are walking into town for an early dinner." Clara paused then flicked a glance up at Amelia. "Do you think we should, um, *wait*? For Jimmy?"

Amelia seemed to consider the question carefully, narrowing her eyes and running a finger over her lower lip. "No. Let's make it a sisters' thing. In fact, I'll text him the address to the motel now."

***

Moments later, Clara had dutifully locked her front door and secured her handbag evenly along her shoulder.

Though Clara enjoyed playing tour guide, Amelia knew Birch Harbor well, if not better.

A warm breeze joined them as they walked and talked, revisiting memories from when Amelia was still at home, living in the big house on the harbor.

Growing up, Clara was less Kate, Amelia, and Megan's younger sister and more the baby of the family. Literally.

Thirteen years as Amelia's junior had set them far apart, though not as distant in age as Clara was with Kate—sixteen years. And while Clara was only ten years younger than Megan, the two were the least close with one another. Clara felt most aligned with Kate—they were both conservative, neat... some might even say *uptight*.

But Clara enjoyed Amelia's company the most. Amelia was fun-loving and easy-going. If Clara worried about something, Amelia would wash it away like sand on the beach.

She'd always been told she was a happy surprise, but Clara's recollections of her youth weren't always so happy. Having an older mother and a long-lost father had thrust Clara into a complicated family dynamic. She knew this.

"It smells like childhood here," Amelia mused, twirling in a circle as they neared Birch Village, a cozy loop of lakeside shops and eateries situated just up from the marina.

Birch Harbor, though small in its year-round population, stretched some miles up and down Lake Huron. Informally, it was divided in two by the broad dock, the harbor the town was named for. South of it, swayed a modest thicket of white Birch trees.

Sometime in the forties, when Birch Harbor gained momentum as a tourist destination, locals dubbed the northwest side of the marina Birch Beach. And surely, it was a lovely beach, attracting daily visitors to spread out on the warm sand, books and bottles of sunscreen tossed casually into the corners of oversized terry cloth towels.

One afternoon at that beach and you'd think you washed ashore at some resort on the Atlantic coast. Show tunes wafted from storefronts along a small boardwalk and the buzz of jet skis and speed boats were just enough to lull you into a lazy nap.

The southeast side of the marina, which saw less economic and tourist activity, took on the moniker Heirloom Cove. Decidedly quieter and less peopled, water from the lake crossed a craggier shoreline and splashed up against rocky outcroppings there. It was a curve of land that offered less beach. In fact, the only beach property there was private. It belonged to the Heirloom Cove homes. A smattering of old teetering waterfront houses. The houses that had once belonged to Birch Harbor settlers. Like, for instance, the Hannigans and the Actons.

Clara followed Amelia's gaze south, toward the cove. "I think my childhood smelled different from yours," Clara murmured. It wasn't meant to be sad or melodramatic, but that's how it came out.

Amelia stopped and tore her eyes away from the house on the harbor. "Was it lonely?"

Clara frowned. "What? You mean growing up there without you?" She studied their old home, the one Clara had left the day after graduating from high school.

"Yeah. Is that what you mean? Your childhood 'smelled different.'" A wry smile curled across Amelia's lips, and Clara grew aware she was being teased.

She laughed at herself a little. "Well, I don't know if I was *lonely*. But there sure was a lot of cleaning. I felt like that's all we did. All *I* did. Your childhood smelled like summer on the lake. Mine smelled like furniture polish."

Amelia didn't laugh.

Instead, they stood together in silence, admiring the old Hannigan house. The one with a dock that sank like a ramp into the lake. The one obscured by sinewy, gray tree trunks and vibrant green leaves. From where they stood, at the crest of a slight hill from which they could tumble into Birch Harbor Bakehouse, the old Hannigan house looked normal. Beautiful, even.

But Clara knew better.

Chapter 4—Megan

Megan had planned to drive into Birch Harbor early the next morning.

But Megan Stevenson was *not* a morning person.

And, more to the point, Brian had the day off. And he was there, in their house. Still refusing to move out. Still sleeping in the guest room. Still in a stand-off about *who* was getting *what*.

The lawyers—his and hers—how cute—were waiting on him to commit to a settlement. Either he put up alimony and child support or Megan got the house.

It was as fair as the snow was white.

But Megan *knew* Brian. Well. His line of business was volatile. Investing in and mining cryptocurrency carried high highs and low lows. It was in Brian's best interest to have *something* stable. The house would be the stability he'd need.

Yet, Megan had stayed in that house for years in her official capacity as the homemaker. *See?* She literally *made* the home. How could he *not* give it to her?

Besides, Megan had no resume, no college degree, and no useful way to earn a living. Sure, Megan had *interests*. She secretly loved romance books and tearjerker movies, though less for the romance and more for the high drama.

She couldn't get enough trashy reality television shows, especially the matchmaking-type. Megan had even been known to personally set up other suburban couples. Some had told her she ought to open a matchmaking business. What a pipe dream.

Unfortunately, romance and *casual* matchmaking among her girlfriends didn't bring in cash.

Therefore, with zero career prospects, Megan needed the house *more* than Brian. Or at least, she needed enough of a monthly stipend to cover the mortgage on a *new* house while she chipped away at figuring out what the heck it was she was going to do with her life. Part-time, dead-end jobs were not calling her name.

For now, having to share space with ol' Brian was physically painful for her. So, she figured she would take the opportunity to bunk up with Clara and Amelia.

A little sisterly surprise. They all needed that, really.

With Sarah securely planted at a friend's house for a last minute-sleepover, Megan drove to Birch Harbor one night early, scrolling through radio stations for most of the drive. Finally, twenty minutes out from her destination, she settled on an audio book.

Meditation in the Car.

It kind of worked.

By the time she rolled into the parking lot of The Bungalows, Clara's five-plex, Megan was so annoyed with trying to hold her breath for extended intervals that she'd nearly forgotten about her messy almost-divorce.

She grabbed her overnight bag from her passenger seat and pushed out of the car and up the cobblestone path toward Unit Two.

Three sets of three sharp raps later, Megan set her bag down and withdrew her phone.

Clara answered on the first ring, predictably. "Megan?" Surprise filled her voice.

"The one-and-only."

Clara let out a sigh. "Is everything okay?"

"Other than the fact that I'm literally living with the person who should, by now, be my EX-husband, everything is perfect. Oh, and... where *are* you?"

Clara answered loudly over a throb of fuzzy background noise. "We're at Fiorillo's in Birch Village. Amelia's here, too."

Megan smiled. Fiorillo's was one of her favorite restaurants in the whole world. It was fate. "Pull up a third chair. I'm less than a mile away."

***

"I see you finally took off your ring," Amelia pointed out through a mouthful of buttery garlic bread.

Megan smiled wryly and wiggled her fingers at Amelia and Clara as she took a sip of her Syrah. "I know. Took me long enough."

"Did you get a new phone?" Amelia was staring at Megan's small, white device.

She shook her head. "No. Same old model I've had for, what, five years now? Is that really pathetic?"

"I hope not." Amelia chuckled. "It looks exactly like mine and I just got this thing a month ago." She waved her own sleek-faced iPhone at the girls who oohed and ahhed appropriately. "A present from Jimmy," Amelia declared proudly.

Megan thought she saw Clara make a face. She spoke up. "This Jimmy guy, is he the real deal?"

"More to the point," Clara interrupted. "How did he afford *that* if he doesn't have a job?"

Amelia's face reddened, and Megan frowned.

"Well, he has a little income stream from an uncle or something. I don't really know the details. But he is *trying* to be the real deal."

"Oh?" Megan asked, lifting an eyebrow.

"He's coming to Birch Harbor. Or, actually, he's *here*. At a motel. Waiting for me."

Clara and Amelia exchanged a look, more of a grimace than a grin, Megan thought.

"Why?" Megan asked, her tone sharp.

"I'm sorry." Amelia shifted in her seat and took a sip of wine. "I just texted him and told him to drop Dobi off later tonight. But he's staying at the motel. Don't worry about him barging in on us." She flicked a glance to Clara. "I think he's bored in the city. And, Jimmy really does love me." Again she wagged the phone in her hand.

"Sounds like a dead end to me," Megan murmured over the top of her wine glass.

Amelia opened her mouth to protest, but Clara held up a hand. "Can we... *not*? Can we just... enjoy each other? For one night? I never get quality time with my sisters."

Megan changed the conversation. Who wanted to talk about relationships, anyway? They were together in their hometown for their mother's death. That was rough enough. "So, how's work, you two?" She pasted a smile onto her face and took another swig.

Though she wasn't quite ready to admit it, Megan was champing at the bit for a career. Something to give her purpose now that her marriage was over and her daughter was approaching graduation.

A black-clad waiter arrived with their plates. Shrimp scampi for Amelia. Fettuccine Alfredo for Megan. And a Caesar salad—dry—for Clara.

"Tell me that's a joke," Amelia pointed a dark gray-tipped nail at Clara's dinner.

"I'm trying to lose seven pounds." Clara avoided their gazes and took another sip of iced tea.

Megan shrugged. "Aren't we all?" Then she pinched her fork in one hand, spoon in the other, and commenced with twirling and shoveling creamy knots of pasta into her mouth.

"*So*, about work... since you asked." Amelia dabbed her napkin along her lips. "I'm waiting to hear back on a role." She bit her lip and lowered her fork to eye Megan's reaction.

Megan swallowed. "Oh? Do tell."

"Lady Macbeth in *Macbeth*. I mean, that's my goal. I think the audition went well. It wasn't a *formal* audition, but I got to have dinner with the director. During appetizers, I put on my Scottish accent, and apart from a couple awkward slips, I nailed it, frankly. But if they offer me another 'Lady in Waiting Number Seven' I might have a public meltdown, so... there's that."

Clara giggled. Megan smiled and shook her head. "You're no Lady in Waiting; that's true. I can't believe you did an accent at dinner."

"I can believe it," Clara cut in, laughing. The three giggled together then grew silent as they worked on their meals.

After some moments, Clara cleared her throat and spoke again. "But Amelia, what *will* you do if you don't get something big?" It was a sober question, which was why Clara asked it and not Megan. Clara was a sober type of girl who asked sobering types of questions, made even more sober by the fact that she was drinking iced tea (no sweetener) and eating dressing-free, gluten-free salad while her sisters indulged in high-carb dishes and full-bodied reds.

Megan might wear dark clothes and carry a chip on her shoulder, but she was less of a dream crusher than her bright, bouncy, blonde baby sister.

Amelia, for her part, was ready for the question. "If I don't get Lady Macbeth or, at the *minimum*, one of the witches, well… I *will* do something drastic."

Clara gasped. "Like *what*?"

Megan couldn't help but smile. It was nice to be part of someone else's drama, rather than her own.

"That's a good question," Amelia replied, dabbing her mouth again with her napkin and staring out through the window at the lake. Megan followed her gaze.

The sun was setting and coloring the water a brilliant orange. Homesickness swelled in her stomach, as it sometimes did. She looked back to Amelia, curious. "Would you move back here?"

Clara and Amelia both fell silent, as though the question were too big. Too much. Too soon.

The three sisters looked at each other around the table, alternating eye contact until a smile spread between them. Amelia answered at last. "I might."

***

Dinner had finished on a high note, and soon they were giggling back up to Clara's apartment in a line along the sidewalk that ran parallel to Harbor Avenue.

Amelia had walked out of Fiorillo's *with* her wine glass, and it was Clara who caught her, grabbed it, and set it on a low-profile wall just outside the back patio. Clara claimed she'd been humiliated, but she, too, was giggling now.

It occurred to Megan that she hadn't laughed as much in ages. Part of her wanted to blame Brian.

Mostly, though, she blamed herself.

When a person stopped being happy, she ought to do two things: look outside first. Declutter that space. Then, she ought to look inside herself. And clean her own house. And once everything was clean, it would be up to her to choose happiness, rather than blame unhappiness on others.

Megan had often chosen to blame others.

She'd decided not to be happy years earlier, when Brian left software development for the crypto world against her wishes. She decided then that she was not happy, but even worse? She decided to *stay* not happy.

Of course, that unhappiness grew like a fungus in their marriage. Both, in the end, shouldered some of the blame. Brian, for continuing to ignore Megan's desire to *do* something with her life, namely, open a business of some sort. And Megan, for leaving the marriage years earlier—emotionally, at least.

Presently, as her sisters marched ahead of her on the cobblestone steps and into Clara's small apartment, Megan pulled her phone out of her back pocket to check her messages.

Sarah had wished her goodnight.

Brian had replied with a yellow thumbs up emoji (she couldn't shake the habit of telling him she'd made it to town).

And yet, another miniature notification glowed at the top of the screen. Its little white envelope sitting there like a delicious dessert.

It was one she'd save for later.

"I'm taking a shower. And whoever is sharing my bed is taking a shower, too," Clara announced once they were all inside.

Megan glanced up, her face reddening, and she slid the phone back into her jeans and smiled. "I'll take the sofa. But I'm also showering."

Amelia pouted. "I shower in the morning. Come on, Clara. Why does it matter?"

Clara bristled. "I just cleaned my sheets. I want to savor the fresh smell for as long as possible between washes, and I'm positive that your feet stink. You can go first, Amelia. Go on." Clara shooed her down the short hallway but not before Amelia dropped her purse onto the floor by the breakfast bar. A few items tumbled out, but she didn't notice.

Clara bent down and snatched up the purse, setting Amelia's phone on the counter for her.

Megan felt a wave of exhaustion climb up her neck and take root in the base of her head.

"Maybe I *won't* shower." She yawned and perched unsteadily on the arm of the sofa.

"Suit yourself," Clara answered, sweeping two empty cans of Diet Coke off the counter and into the trash before plugging her phone into its charger. "Let's get your bed ready," she suggested to Megan.

Megan stood and stretched, then helped.

Soon enough, Amelia had returned from the shower and Megan had unpacked her essentials—night cream, phone, phone charger, and Kindle—on the counter and was pouring herself a glass of water from a smart looking water pitcher in the fridge.

Amelia reached for her phone, waved half-heartedly, bid Megan goodnight, and saw herself to bed.

Minutes later, as Megan was climbing beneath the sheets with her precious e-Reader, she heard Amelia and Clara in the back of the apartment, their voices raised excitedly.

She tried to ignore the commotion, since a dull headache was taking shape in the center of her forehead. But it was futile, because Amelia came barging down the hall and into the living room, Clara hot on her heels.

"Oh. My. Goodness," Amelia gushed.

Megan craned her neck up to see a broad smile on her sister's face. Then Clara joined, with the opposite expression.

"Oh my goodness is *right*," Clara added, anger flashing in her eyes.

"What's going *on*," Megan demanded, sitting up and rubbing her neck.

"I accidentally grabbed your phone," Amelia sang back, holding out the white-trimmed cellular right in front of Megan's squinting eyes. Amelia jabbered on, amused as could be, "And I'll be darned if this isn't a *dating app*."

Chapter 5—Kate

Rain had begun to fall just *after* Kate tucked herself into Michael Matuszewski's office.

Stupidly, she'd left her umbrella in her car, wedged neatly in the space between her seat and the console.

Rain is a good sign, she reminded herself as she forced a smile for the receptionist.

"You must be... Katherine Hannigan?" the woman greeted.

Kate nodded. "Call me Kate, please. And that would make you Sharon?"

The woman rose and stretched out a small hand. Kate offered hers, and instead of a handshake, Sharon gave her a warm squeeze. "It's nice to formally meet you, Kate. I'm terribly sorry about your mom. You were busy, so I didn't want to pester you, but I came to the wake. You know," Sharon went on chattily, "Nora was in here more than once, squirrelling away money for you girls, no doubt—"

Kate cut the woman off with a terse *thank you* and asked if Michael was ready. It's not that she didn't appreciate Sharon's kindness. It was that kindness made Kate want to cry. And, well... she wasn't too certain she could regain her footing if the floodgates were opened.

Regardless, that day was not a crying day. It was a business day.

"Oh, right. Well, you *are* ten minutes early," Sharon chirped, her merry attitude never faltering. "But I'll let him know you've arrived."

Kate settled into a chair and selected a three-year-old copy of *Martha Stewart* to peruse as Sharon bustled around, poking into Michael's office in the back then watering the plants until finally lowering back behind the mahogany reception desk.

Aware of Sharon's boredom and her own looming anxiety at the fact that her sisters had yet to arrive, Kate cleared her throat. "Thank you for coming to the funeral, Sharon," she said quietly.

"Oh, honey. It was the most beautiful wake I've ever attended. And I've been to my share, I'll have you know. Such tasteful music selections. The floral arrangements... *my*," Sharon gasped. Kate smiled at that and built up enough courage to meet her eyes as she went on, describing elements of the event that Kate had put grief-stricken energy into but didn't quite have the luxury to enjoy, since, well...

"Kate." Michael appeared, his trim, tall build a reassuring presence and his good looks a nice distraction. "I have everything ready. Would you like to come back?" He waved a gentlemanly hand down the hall, and Kate rose from her seat, her back straight as an arrow.

"My sisters are on their way, I'm sure. Should we wait?"

"Sharon will show them in. Right, Sharon?" He flashed a broad grin to his receptionist who nearly melted right there on the spot. Instead, though, she nodded meekly. Kate could relate. Michael was perfection. Always had been. Tanned and toned. Focused and smart. And, successful. He'd make a perfect match for Kate, people had always said.

She didn't agree.

Kate never intended to date again. *But*, if she *did*, it wouldn't be someone like Michael Matuszewski.

It would be someone who laughed at the wrong moments and overslept and wore mismatched socks. Someone who would not remind her of Paul. Someone she could snuggle on the sofa with and who would go for a lazy stroll rather than sign her up for marathons.

It would be someone... softer, who could smooth Kate's rough edges instead of sharpening them into blades.

Michael was a sharpener. He belonged with a woman who craved structure. A woman who needed it.

Kate already had that, and in too much supply.

Moments later they were sitting in his office. Wood and leather everywhere, in typical male fashion. When Kate finally moved from Apple Tree Hill, she would limit the dark and dense in favor of white and light. It was a personal vow.

"How've you been?" Michael asked, lacing his fingers on top of his desk.

Several thick binders lined the edge of the wood, and she wondered exactly what the day would bring. What her mom had in store for them.

Surely, no surprises. Surely it was all as Nora had promised her daughters: an even split. Two paid-off houses, one rental property, and a square slab of farmland. Something for each daughter.

"Knock, knock." Amelia's voice echoed at the doorway. Kate whipped her head around to take in the sorry sight of three, sleepy-eyed younger sisters. A flashback hit—high school. The morning after prom. Kate and Amelia trudging down the stairs to join Nora in the kitchen. A fresh pot of coffee percolating rhythmically, as their mother waited as though she knew. Embarrassment had colored Kate's teenage cheeks. Excitement colored Amelia's.

But Amelia hadn't been a tattletale. Not then or ever.

Now, Kate reminded herself that she was *not* her mother. She smiled at her sisters, realizing Megan happened to come to town the night before, after all.

"Michael, you remember Amelia, Megan, and Clara?" Kate asked.

He stood and adjusted his tie along his flat abdomen. Kate glanced away, only to catch Amelia's eyes narrowing.

"Michael," Amelia answered airily. She didn't sound like herself.

Megan and Clara hung by the door as Amelia rolled her shoulders back and took the seat at the other end of the semi-circle, nearest Michael's desk.

Michael, oblivious, gestured to the two empty seats.

Kate pressed a hand to her head and tried to refocus them. "Megan, Clara, come sit." They did as they were told, and Kate waved Michael on, granting him permission to begin.

Before he sat back down, Michael picked up the folders and passed one to each sister.

Kate ran her hand over the leather, her index finger tracing the gold-embossed *MM* in the center.

Inside each binder was a packet of legalese—jargon about probate proceedings and estate affairs and case law *this* and precedent *that*. Nothing personal to Nora's accounts or plans.

Michael rambled on about usual procedure as the women shuffled through pages that read, to them, like stereo instructions.

Megan interrupted. "Any chance you can cut to the chase, Michael?"

He looked up, no doubt unaware that four lives sat there before him.

A woman whose husband died and who had no more money to cover the mortgage.

A woman with no real job and a vapid life in a city she hardly called home.

A woman in the throes of divorce with a child at home still.

And a young woman whose life had yet to really begin.

Kate glanced at Clara to see how she was doing. She seemed okay, so Kate helped soften Megan's blow by addressing Michael softly. "We're tired and sad. And, maybe anxious." She glanced more pointedly at her sisters.

Megan sighed.

Amelia, too.

Michael cleared his throat. "Of course, of course. Again, I'm so sorry for your loss. I'll get down to it, I suppose."

Kate leaned forward slightly. Clara did the same.

"In your mother's last will and testament, she determined Katherine Acton Hannigan would act as executor. In the event that Katherine, or Kate," he looked up briefly at Kate and smiled, "is unable to fulfill the duties, the role of executor falls to Amelia-Ann Hannigan. And then, to Megan Beth Hannigan." He paused again, and the women nodded.

Clara kept mum.

"Nora Katherine Hannigan signed and sealed her last will and testament recently, I'd like to add."

Amelia lifted an eyebrow. "Had she become a frequent flier in here?"

He shook his head. "She visited from time to time, yes. Chatting with Sharon out there," he paused to nod toward the waiting room warmly before going on, "but in terms of formal changes, she handled the last one with a former associate of mine. Zack Durbin worked here for a short time and handled your mother's estate." He shifted in his seat, and Kate sensed a nervousness, though why she couldn't imagine.

Megan added, "I didn't know she updated it at all. Didn't she settle this back in the nineties after Clara was born?"

Kate shushed everyone. "Michael clearly has this information right in front of him," she said to her sisters.

"I want to caution you all," Michael answered. Kate blinked. Amelia frowned. He went on, "Many families enter these meetings with an idea of how things will go. Sometimes, the decedent has been crystal clear, and there are no hiccups. More often than not, however, the survivors don't always know *everything*." Both his words and tone were ominous, but it didn't quite reach Kate. As though she were stuck in a trance—a belief—that her mother had done precisely what she'd told them she would do, she batted his warning away.

"I'm sure it's fine. Go ahead, Michael. *Please.*"

Chapter 6—Clara

One Year Earlier.

"She's over seventy now, and, from the sounds of it, her symptoms started years ago. So, no. It's not early onset," the doctor replied. Clara watched Kate nod in response. She watched her keep it together, her eyes dry, her gaze steady.

Then, Clara looked at her mom, whose face was blank.

"So," Clara inserted herself through trembled speech, "what does the prognosis look like?"

The doctor cleared his throat and laced his fingers on his desk. Glimmering windows of other high-rise buildings shone like the broad sides of diamonds behind him.

Clara hated the city. Even more now. Big cities meant bad news.

"It varies," he answered Clara, then turned to speak directly to her mom. "Mrs. Hannigan—"

"It's *Miz*," Nora corrected, her voice a sheet of ice.

He flushed, Clara was certain. She couldn't help but smile. It was the exact sort of thing to level the tension. Clara glanced at Kate and they shared the sentiment, silently. Some relief.

"Excuse me. *Miz* Hannigan. To answer your question, this disease looks different for different people. For all we know, you could live a normal life for another twenty years."

Clara could have sworn Kate sucked in a sharp breath.

The doctor went on. "Or, it could progress quickly. The best we can do is schedule regular appointments. Keep up with the meds. Eat well. Stay active. The whole bit." He raised his palms and smiled. White teeth glowed back at them. Clara's own smile fell away. Doctors liked to use "we" as though they had any control over the diseases they diagnosed or the patients they treated.

Little did this one know, Nora Hannigan would not be controlled. By his treatment plan, the medications, good nutrition, or anything else.

But, again, their mom didn't seem to react at all. The only moment that perked her up was when the doctor accused her of being married.

"What's next?" Kate asked, poising her pen above a notepad trimmed in a floral pattern.

"Truthfully?" he asked, now frowning and pulling his rimless glasses down his nose and folding them neatly. Kate and Clara nodded together on either side of their mother. He went on. "Make the most of your time together. Keep her healthy," he pointed his forehead toward the older woman, speaking—once again—about her rather than to her. "And," he added, his voice dropping an octave, "start making preparations."

***

"Mom, you said hardly a word in there," Clara pointed out as they ushered her into Kate's Navigator.

Nora clicked her tongue. "Do you believe even one word that man said?" she hissed, pulling herself into the front seat with Clara's help.

"What's not to believe, Mom?" Kate asked. "And also, are we still going to Fiorillo's for lunch?"

Clara frowned at her older sister. "How can you think about eating right now?"

"I'll tell you how," Kate answered, bristling as she launched into a classic Kate lecture. "Nothing has changed. Absolutely nothing has changed. People go to the doctor and learn something new then let that *news* disrupt their lives. We won't. Right, Mom?"

Nora came to life. She spoke lucidly and with focus. "I agree with Kate. Just because he confirmed what you two suspected doesn't mean I'm going to walk into Lake Huron with rocks in my coat pockets. Fiorillo's is perfect. We need wine. If you want to know my mind, well, I think doctors see people like me and haven't a clue what to think. What they ought to do is put in a prescription for a bottle of wine. The good stuff. It'd save us all money and time and headaches."

Clara smiled in the backseat and shook her head, catching Kate's amused face in the rearview mirror. "Well, *wine* won't save you a headache, but I do see your point."

Their mom twisted to face Clara, her hand gripping the console to keep her body in its awkward position. Clara's eyes hung on the baubles clacking between Nora's knobby knuckles. Glinting silvers and golds that made the woman who she was. A glamour girl. A Titaness.

A small-town queen crashing into her golden years like she was late to her own party.

But beneath the gems lay paper-thin, age-spotted skin. Prematurely bruised. Arthritic. The product of a life built on hard work rather than precious jewels and luxury. The latter two were the result of a cutthroat attitude and decades of ruthless business building. *The spoils of war*, their mom often sang out as she swung a glimmering fist across her chest.

"A wine headache is different than a bad news headache," the woman murmured with a wink before turning back around and directing Kate where to go, unnecessarily.

***

Lunch was a fast affair. Salad all around. Basket of garlic bread untouched.

"Doggy-bag these," Nora directed the waiter.

Clara offered a smile after her mother and thanked him discreetly. "*Mom*," she began, only to think better of reprimanding the poor woman for her typically absent manners. It wouldn't be productive.

"What? Trudy loves scraps."

"You shouldn't feed Trudy people food, Mom. You know that," Kate replied, slipping her card out of the check holder and tucking it back into her leather wallet. "She's already overweight."

Nora ignored Kate and took the box from the waiter, adding a syrupy thank you, after all.

Clara wondered about that. Not the boxed garlic bread destined for a cruel, fat-bellied Chihuahua, but about her mom's insincerity, swinging from overweening demands to gushing supplication in the blink of an eye.

Had the woman *always* been disingenuous? Or was it a recent development? Clara couldn't tell anymore. It was as if her own memory had turned fuzzy, too.

"Where to next, ladies?" Clara asked with a yawn, checking her wristwatch. She had papers to grade and a kitchen to clean. Both responsibilities she'd no doubt put off when she actually arrived back home.

She'd once read somewhere that true perfectionists were also procrastinators. They hated to tackle a chore for fear of, well, imperfect execution. Maybe Clara ought to lower her personal standards.

It might pay off in more ways than she knew.

"Home. Right, Mom?" Kate asked once they were situated in the SUV.

Nora pointed up the hill toward Main Street. "No, take me to see Michael."

Clara flashed a glance to the rearview, locking eyes with Kate. They frowned at each other. "Michael? As in, Michael Matuszewski?" Kate replied.

Their mom nodded. "Yes. He's my lawyer."

"I know that, Mom. Why do you want to see him?"

"I have to fix something. Sign something. He called the other day and wanted to go over a document. Just stop complaining and take me there, goldarn it, Kate."

Kate's eyes grew wide in the mirror and Clara let out a sigh.

They arrived at the attorney's office, and Nora let herself out of the SUV. Kate and Clara opened their doors too, but the old woman held up a hand and stopped them. "I'll be five minutes. Just stay there," she commanded.

Again, the sisters exchanged a look. Clara shook her head. "We have to go with her, right?"

Kate nodded. "Mom, we're coming with you."

"Five minutes!" Nora screeched as she tugged the door open and waddled inside before they could stop her.

True to her word, Nora emerged at the door again in just five minutes. This time, with a plump, cheery-looking woman gabbing away at her side who waved boisterously at Kate and Clara.

She walked Nora to the Navigator and said *hello* and *nice day out* and all the things chatty types couldn't help but eject despite the circumstances.

"Everything go okay in there, Mom?" Kate helped Nora buckle her seatbelt then waited for an answer. The air conditioning hummed softly around them.

"It went well." Nora stared straight ahead. Her jaw slack, her breathing heavy for such a short excursion. "I just had to drop something off."

Clara's skin prickled. "You said you were signing a document."

"Did I?"

"Yes, Mom," Kate answered.

"Well, no. I had to drop something off. I don't want to talk about it. I need to rest now." Nora's flame had started to flicker. It was the emerging normal. A full day of high energy and feisty bossiness that eventually, come early afternoon, waned into a sludge.

As they crested the hill back down Harbor Avenue, Nora lifted a wobbly finger out toward Heirloom Cove. "Have you watered the flowers lately, Kate?" she asked quietly.

Kate glanced at Clara before replying. "Clara does that now, Mom. Remember? She's the one who takes care of the old house."

Nora lifted a painted eyebrow then lowered it. "Oh, right. Well, Clara?" she twisted in her seat part of the way and dropped her chin. "Have you?"

"Yep. I was there Tuesday. Speaking of which," Clara took a risk. It was something she and Kate and even Amelia and Megan had been arguing about for ages. It was something they'd better settle sooner rather than later. "What are we doing with the house, Mom?"

"What do you mean?"

Kate looked over at Nora.

Clara forged ahead. "I mean, when are we going to start clearing it out?"

The old house on the harbor had all but turned into a museum by that point.

"You can handle it after I'm dead," their mom replied, flatly.

Clara's pulse quickened and she unbuckled from the middle seat in the back, feeling suddenly like a little girl all over again. An eavesdropper on a conversation that didn't belong to her.

But it did.

"Mom. *Not* okay," Clara reprimanded.

The woman batted her hand weakly. "You can sort through everything then. Right, Kate?"

Both Kate and Clara drew back at the question. Clara waited for Kate to say something—anything—to diminish the morbid thought and also take back the reins.

Kate blew out a sigh. "Oh, Mom. Do you have any idea how much work that will be? And how difficult? We will already be sad, then we have to face all of your *things*? Your belongings? We really should start *now* while—"

"While I'm alive and you're still irritated with me instead of when I'm dead and you feel guilty about pestering me." Nora coughed into her fist, a dry, phony cough.

Clara rolled her eyes. "Whatever."

Kate let out a short laugh. "Something like that," she answered, laying her hand over their mother's on the console.

They rolled past the old place, and Nora leaned forward in her seat, craning her neck around Kate to get a better view.

"Do you want to go there now, Mom?" Clara asked from between the two front seats, her voice soft.

The SUV heaved forward as Kate took her foot off the brake and checked her rearview mirror, this time looking beyond Clara.

Nora fell back into her seat and crossed her arms like a petulant child. "No. Keep driving, Katherine. I will never step a foot in that haunted place again."

"Mom, whoa. *Haunted*?" Clara asked, confused by the woman's sudden shift.

"I don't want to talk about it. With either one of you. Don't take me there. Don't bury me there. Don't even drag my casket into the front parlor there."

Clara and Kate fell quiet. All of their lives, Nora loved the old house on Heirloom Cove. As far as they knew, that's why Nora kept it instead of selling or renting.

But, her words stuck. As addled as Nora's mind may have been, Clara and Kate solemnly and silently vowed to fulfill her wish.

Nora Hannigan would never go back to the house on the harbor.

And Clara began to wonder why.

Chapter 7—Amelia

Tucking a strand of her dark hair behind her ear, Amelia leaned in toward Michael, ready to devour every word.

Though there was nothing specific Amelia hoped to have *earned* from her mother's estate, she was very interested in how things worked out. Who got what. As a middle child, she had always been acutely aware of discrepancies.

Inequities.

Imbalances.

Now, Amelia knew, those things would be revealed in full.

Her phone buzzed in her purse on the floor. Jimmy, no doubt. She'd told him they could meet for lunch in the Village, and it was his own fault if he couldn't entertain himself in the meantime.

Although, Amelia figured he'd find *something* to do. Jimmy was that type. He made friends easily. Didn't mind putting himself out there. He should have been a car salesman, probably, rather than a construction worker. He loved meeting new people and getting into trouble. Two things that had drawn Amelia to him to begin with.

The friendly bad boy, Megan had once dubbed Amelia's "type."

She pushed her bag with her toe to muffle the buzzing and returned her attention to the lawyer.

Michael cleared his throat. "We'll begin with your mother's personal effects. Then, I'll share her wishes regarding real estate." When no one reacted, he read on, quoting their mom. "'To Katherine, I leave twenty-three flowerpots, my dining room table, the front hall runner, my wedding china, Wendell Acton's wristwatch, and my Sunday wardrobe.'"

Amelia leaned back, studying her older sister's face and then glancing to catch Megan and Clara's reactions.

Kate's throat bobbed in a swallow and her chest rose and fell.

Clara blinked and tucked her lips inside her teeth.

Megan shrugged.

Pausing, Michael lowered the page from which he read, perhaps waiting for the inevitable. An argument. A passive aggressive sigh. Anything.

"I didn't know she named her clothes by the day of the week," Kate answered softly.

A small giggle erupted among the girls. Amelia knew if their mom was there, she'd snap at them for making fun. But a little laughter was just what the doctor ordered. The whole affair had become too tense. Too awkward.

Amelia added, "I hope I get Saturday."

Again, they laughed together in front of poor Michael, who appeared unsure how to react.

"Go ahead, keep reading," Kate said at last, wiping away happy tears. Or maybe sad. Amelia couldn't tell which anymore.

He held the paper back up to his face and answered, "That concludes Kate's inheritance of Nora's personal effects."

Amelia blinked and raised her eyebrows at her older sister. But Kate simply smiled. "Right. I expected as much."

Michael continued. "Shall I go on?"

All four sisters nodded urgently, and so he did.

"'To Amelia,'" he began. Amelia leaned forward again and narrowed her eyes on Michael's full lips behind the thick, white page. "'I leave the upstairs chaise, my patio furniture, Wendell Acton's Smith and Wesson snub nose, Aunt Ida's tiger's eye necklace, and… '" Amelia sucked in a breath. "'My furs.'"

"*Furs*?" Clara cried out.

Amelia sank back, oddly disappointed, though not necessarily in her mother's fashion choices.

Michael stopped reading and set the page down.

Kate murmured that she didn't know Nora *had* any furs and that she figured any guns were long gone.

Clara carried on about how they ought to donate any fur—if, in fact, Nora owned any *real* fur— to animal shelters to be used as beds. "Fur is beyond passé. It's unethical," she added, clicking her tongue in disgust.

Megan yawned.

"Donate them," Amelia spat. "I don't want fur coats. And why does she refer to Dad by his full name?" She crossed her arms and shook her head before adding, "I'm sorry, Michael. Go ahead with the will. I just—"

"You had different expectations," he answered patiently. It's understandable. Amelia bit her lower lip and glanced up at him to catch a look. An unreadable, un-lawyerly *look*.

"Yes. Silly, really. Just go ahead."

The women sighed collectively, and he did as he was told.

"'To Megan, I leave my silver Tiffany's collection, my wedding band, Wendell Acton's wedding band, the desktop computer, and our marital bed.'"

"I guess we know who the favorite is," Amelia muttered, lifting a conspiratorial eyebrow to Clara, who ignored her.

"Her 'desktop computer'?" Megan turned her head sharply to Amelia. "As in the 'new' one she got in 2000 once she was convinced Y2K 'killed' her old one?" Megan rolled her eyes.

Clara made a face. "What does she mean by *marital* bed?"

Michael offered a sympathetic smile, but it was Kate who answered. "Obviously the king bed that was in her bedroom."

"Why did she have to use the word *marital*?" Clara asked again, but it was Amelia this time who added a dose of maturity.

"Mom was trying to be specific, no doubt. Go ahead, Michael." Amelia bit down on her thumbnail, anxiety creeping in.

Michael lifted his eyebrows, waiting for permission to read. Amelia rolled her hand in a wide circle to get him going again.

"'The balance of my personal possessions is to be divided evenly under the supervision of my eldest daughter, Katherine.'"

Four jaws dropped.

It was a bombshell.

An error.

An oversight.

Kate spoke immediately. "What about Clara?" she asked, glancing wildly from her sisters to Michael.

He shook his head. "No personal items were specifically designated to Clara Hannigan."

"Is there more?" Amelia asked, trying to be helpful.

"Yes, her properties and a personal letter."

"Okay, then go ahead," Amelia prompted. Kate nodded her head, and Megan and Clara did the same, all four of them frowning deeply.

"All right," he answered. "'Real estate and land, including owned and leased properties, businesses, and accounts related thereto,'" Michael continued, holding a new page crisply between himself and the women. His eyes danced down to Nora's own words, and he read, "'As for my rental properties, including the Birch Creek Cottage, The Bungalows, and the undeveloped parcel inland, I would ask they be evenly divided between Katherine, Amelia, and Megan.'"

Amelia felt her stomach twist with stress.

She glanced over at Clara, expecting a fresh round of tears. Anger. The exact feelings that Amelia had felt many times over during the course of her own upbringing.

But Clara's face was expressionless. Calm.

Clara and Kate exchanged their own glance, and that's when Amelia realized why Clara wasn't having a tantrum right then and there.

The house.

The house on the harbor.

Chapter 8—Megan

Megan wasn't easily rattled.

But something didn't sit right.

Nora had updated her will recently. So why wasn't Clara named? And why wasn't the house included?

The scowl on Amelia's face suggested exactly what Megan was thinking, but there wasn't a chance. It was their family home. The place they'd grown up in. No way would their own mother leave the whole thing to Clara.

Then again, knowing Nora, perhaps it *did* make sense.

"Is she getting the house?" Megan asked point blank, her finger aimed directly at the youngest of the group, Megan's black nail polish providing a sort of morbid costume effect in the context of the probate meeting.

Michael opened his mouth to answer but Clara beat him to the punch. "I certainly hope so. Don't you think it would be nice if she thought I was worth *something*?" She brushed her blonde hair back over her shoulder, and Megan saw a flush creeping up her youngest sister's neck, blossoming into her cheeks.

Clara was such a child. Still.

"It wouldn't be fair for you to get the Heirloom house, Clara. Surely you can see that," Megan hissed, feeling herself lose control.

The whole meeting had been a disappointment. An uncomfortable, awkward disappointment, peppered only by brief moments of humor that were quickly washed away by the revelation that Nora Hannigan hand-selected her oldest daughter to play Mom and divvy out scraps to the others. And for *Clara* to get the *house*? Unconscionable.

Kate raised a flat palm. "Enough. We have no idea what becomes of the Heirloom house, because Michael hasn't gotten that far. And if Clara *doesn't* get it, then we still have an issue."

"What issue?" Amelia piped up. Megan nodded sagely in agreement over the question.

"What *issue*? The issue of one of us being left out of the will, obviously," Kate answered. "Especially the one who has been caretaker to both Mom and the house, itself, for years now. *Years*," she emphasized, "while you, you, and even *I* have been out living our lives beyond the borders of Birch Harbor, I might remind you." Kate thrust a bare index finger first at Megan then at Amelia and finally at herself as she rounded out her argument.

Megan dropped her gaze. Amelia kept mum. Michael cleared his throat for what felt like the millionth time. If Megan had to hear him do it again then she was leaving. Her mother and father's marital bed was not worth all this. Especially considering their father had *left* them.

"Nora included a separate declaration for the Heirloom Cove property," Michael said at last, his voice as even and earnest as could be. "Her final wish."

The women looked with interest at him, each sitting tightly on the edge of her seat.

"Is this the part she updated recently?"

"Yes and no," Michael admitted at last, pressing his lips into a line before adding, "The last time Nora was here was for a separate matter. A... *private* matter." His eyes darted up to Kate, who seemed confused. "But she did have the opportunity to confirm the plans for her personal effects and various properties."

Amelia pushed air through her lips, and Megan clapped her hands on her thighs. "Classic Nora," she snorted, rising and tugging her handbag onto her shoulder.

"Megan, *please*," Kate whispered.

But Megan couldn't take it. Not after all they'd been through. Not after the reading of the will and the notable favoritism apparent between Nora and Kate, and now probably Clara, too.

Amelia reached for Megan and rested her hand on her arm, pulling her gently back to her seat. "Megan, it's fine. We have no idea what's in there. We're in this together, remember?" The two locked eyes and Megan felt a sob crawl up her throat.

Her own divorce. Nora's death. It was all too much.

But Amelia was right.

They were sisters.

Kate, Amelia, Megan, and Clara.

They were sisters.

No matter what happened, they'd make things right.

Even if eccentric, bitter, game-playing Nora Hannigan had set things wrong.

Chapter 9—Kate

"'Regarding 131 Harbor Avenue, the property and land situated on Heirloom Cove and the private beach included in said parcel,'" Michael read, his voice clear and even, as though whatever might be wrapped up in their mother's written words needed a stable platform, a firm channel. Kate felt her breaths grow quick and shallow. She glanced at her sisters, each on the edge of her seat. "'Upon my death, I leave the deed to be transferred to Katherine Nora Hannigan, Amelia Ann Hannigan, and Megan Beth Stevenson.'"

Kate gasped.

Their mother's language was crisp and precise. The content of her final wish relevant and painfully recent. As recent as Megan's wedding, at the very least. As recent as Nora's eventual acceptance that Megan chose to take Brian's last name, in an inflammatory act of daughterly defiance.

Michael set the page down.

No one said a word.

The silence continued on for some moments. Uncomfortable and suffocating.

Clara was the next to emit a stifled sound. A soft sob.

Kate glanced at Amelia and Megan, who were dutifully confused. Respectfully quiet.

"Are you serious?" Amelia whispered to Michael.

He nodded.

Kate stood. "Let me see, please." She stretched a hand out as Amelia and Megan reached over to their littlest sister.

Michael lowered his voice. "Kate," he said, "it would be best if you and I meet privately. I have one more item for you to go over as the executor. But we need to look at it alone." He glanced beyond her to the others.

Kate nodded and turned.

"Let's take a break first," she suggested, exhaustion pooling at the base of her neck. She pushed a finger to each temple.

The others rose and paused as if to thank Michael. But it was hard to show gratitude on the heels of bad news.

Michael stood to walk the ladies out of the office. He stopped in the hall when Kate turned to address him one last time for that morning.

"When should I come back?" she asked plainly.

"I have no obligations for the rest of the day. I knew the Hannigan Estate—your mother's estate—would be... "

"A challenge?" she finished his sentence.

Nodding gravely, he added, "All estates present obstacles. Death is hard. And handling the affairs of the deceased amplifies that. Nora, of course, had a lot to decide. That's never easy. Not even for a sharp-witted, good woman like your mom."

His words should have hit the right notes. They should have reassured her.

But Kate knew her own mother too well. She thanked Michael and followed her sisters outside into the warmth of the early summer sun.

Humidity hadn't yet set in, or perhaps, hadn't yet made its way to their position inland.

"What are we going to do?" Amelia asked, her face scrunched in fret.

Megan replied, "Do you mean about the will or—?"

"Of course I mean the will. What else?" the former snapped.

Clara shook her head sadly, blinking against the rays of late morning light that cut across the parking lot. Kate pulled her sunglasses from her handbag and took over. "Lunch. The Harbor Deli. We'll talk there. In the meantime, just let it settle. Clara, why don't you ride with me?"

"I drove them here," Clara whined, hooking a thumb at Amelia and Megan as though they were aggravating teenagers to be trucked from activity to activity.

Kate considered the next best route. She'd have to return to Michael's office and intended to do so sooner rather than later. But she didn't want Amelia or Megan to get into Clara's head.

Or, worse, spill any beans.

Lord knew there were plenty to spill.

Kate assumed that Nora had spent extra time at Michael's because she was taking care to arrange her affairs tightly and without issue. The woman never once asked for help. She never once suggested anything would be... unexpected.

Yet there they were, four sisters. Four properties. But only three claims.

It was like a sick and twisted nursery rhyme. A riddle. One Kate couldn't solve.

Or, more likely, *refused* to solve.

Because the only explanation was the truth.

And the truth, the Hannigan truth, would change everything.

***

Amelia and Megan ended up riding with Kate. Clara drove alone. They met at the deli and each ordered some version of a turkey sandwich. Iced teas all around.

The lake lapped up against the boats in the marina, just yards away from their bistro table on the patio. Kate wanted nothing more than to sit there and enjoy the view she'd given up years back, when she decided to become a suburban housewife. A mom with a backyard that was many miles away from the threat of an open body of water.

"What's the deal?" Amelia asked, once they had all settled in with their sandwiches and clinking glasses of amber beverage.

Kate let out a deep sigh and leaned forward on her elbows. "The deal is that Mom obviously went senile earlier than we realized."

Megan lifted a dark eyebrow and took a small bite of her lunch, covering her mouth with a napkin as she held Kate's gaze.

"Right?" Kate asked. A heavy frown set on her mouth, pulling the skin of her cheeks with it. She propped her face in her hands and could feel her age, pooling there, where her jawline was starting to become jowls. She felt old. Old and stupid. And, alone. Even among her sisters.

Perhaps, especially among her sisters.

Megan looked away. Amelia kept quiet.

Kate felt her stomach clench, and she set her sandwich down. "Clara, what time do you have to get back to work?"

"I have a substitute until lunch. So, soon. Half an hour. Tops," she replied, studying her wristwatch for an extra beat.

"Right, well. Here's the plan." Kate rubbed her fingertips into a clean paper napkin and took a sip of tea for courage. "I'll go back to the office—Michael's office—and see about filing an appeal, or whatever it is you do.

"To contest the will?" Megan chimed in.

"Yes, to contest the will. Do you all agree?"

Clara buried her face in her hands and nodded her head.

Amelia and Megan murmured their agreement.

"Good. It's settled. This is clearly a case of a woman gone mad. I'm sure our biggest obstacle will be Michael, himself. Clearly he didn't put two-and-two together sooner and *guide* Mom."

"Woman gone mad," Amelia muttered into the wind as she stared out across the water below them.

Just on the other side of the marina sat the house. Heirloom Cove, with its rocky shoreline and long shadows, stood darkly against the glimmering water. The small figure of the old house, its red paint glowing from between white birch trees, taunted them.

Kate looked at Clara, who was also staring at the house.

She spoke, at last. "I don't know how I'll ever go back there," Clara whispered.

Megan snorted. "I don't blame you."

"Let's just leave it be. Mom made a mistake. That much is clear."

"No," Clara replied. "I have a feeling she didn't make a mistake. I think she made a point."

Chapter 10—Amelia

Like the leftovers of a strong perfume, Clara's fear hung in the air long after she had excused herself to return to work.

The others remained on the patio as the sun drifted up as high in the sky as it would go.

Amelia traced doodles into the condensation on her iced tea. Megan scrolled through her phone. Kate stared off—at the lake or the house, Amelia wasn't sure.

"It was a mistake," the oldest one said at last.

Amelia and Megan looked at each other, and Amelia saw something flicker behind Megan's eyes. Sympathy? Or, the opposite?

As Amelia opened her mouth to reply that, no, it clearly was *not* a mistake, something else caught her attention. A figure, tall and lean, striding comfortably beneath the easy layer of a graphic tee-shirt and khaki shorts—the exact opposite of what one would expect a construction worker to wear—toward the patio. His thick blonde hair bounced with style on his head.

Jimmy.

Amelia closed her eyes and pressed her hand into her forehead, but it was too late.

"Amelia!" he called loudly and waved.

Megan pulled her sunglasses down her nose and narrowed her gaze on him. Kate turned and covered her eyes with her hand, squinting into the wash of sunlight that spread beyond their bistro umbrella. "Who's that?" she asked.

Amelia plastered a fake smile on her face, stood, smoothed her shirt, and opened her hands. "Jimmy?" she feigned pleasant surprise. "What are you *doing* here?"

"Babe," he cooed, smiling at the other deli patrons as he strolled past slowly. When he arrived at their table, Amelia felt herself sway back slightly. But he slipped his hands around her waist and pulled her to him in a deep hug. The type of hug that had, months earlier, persuaded her to start seeing him.

The type that got her into trouble.

He pressed a wet kiss on her cheek and spun her around to face her sisters. "Lunch, right?" Jimmy said, dipping his chin in a pout. "But I see you started without me."

"Is this the construction boyfriend?" Megan asked.

Amelia flushed and her eyes grew wide. "Megan," she hissed. "Do you have an ounce of tact?"

But Jimmy didn't care. He loved it. "I *am* the construction boyfriend," he answered with a broad smile. "Jimmy Baker, at your service. I dabble in a little bit of everything. Framing, electric, plumbing. If I had a card, I'd give you one." He stuck out a strong, smooth hand—the sort of hand that did not belong to a *successful* laborer. Amelia knew this deep inside, and she winced.

Kate hesitated a second too long before offering her hand to Jimmy in return. But, still, she offered it, and he ignored the delay. "Kate?" he asked.

"That's right," she answered.

It occurred to Amelia just then that Jimmy thought of himself as a charmer, a suave playboy type able to win over any woman, anywhere. It had worked on her, after all.

But he hadn't met Amelia's sisters.

"And that's Megan," Amelia pointed across the table, willing him to disappear inside, where he could order a decaf coffee and chat up the sandwich maker for half an hour.

After nodding and even bowing slightly toward the farthest seated sister, he lingered. "Am I interrupting anything?"

Amelia felt her heart tug a little, and she smiled. "Well," she began, looking at Kate for guidance.

"No," Kate answered, surprising them all. "No, Jimmy. Please, sit. You'll be a good distraction, actually." She offered a warm, motherly smile, and Amelia wondered if she was wrong about Jimmy. He meant well, after all.

And he was fun.

And sweet.

And hot.

Too hot, probably.

Jimmy pulled Amelia's chair out and gestured for her to take a seat before easing himself into Clara's empty spot.

"This town is great," he began, before launching into a full-blown review of all he'd seen. "It doesn't smell like fish guts or bird poop, unlike the lake in the town where I grew up."

The women relaxed, Kate even letting a short laugh escape her mouth. "Oh yeah?"

"Oh yeah," he replied. "And here," he waved a hand around Birch Village, "not too many people but enough to make it interesting. And there's a beach. Who knew you could find ocean-front property in Michigan?"

He went on and on, complimenting the variety of eateries and shops for their quaint effect, the motel for how clean the bathroom was, and asking, at last, what the plan was for the day.

"Well," Amelia started, genuinely sorry to break the bad news to him. "We aren't sure yet. There's been a hang-up."

"With the will?" Jimmy asked, his tone thickening.

Kate straightened her back and took a long sip of tea. Megan set her phone down for the first time in ten minutes.

"Yeah," Amelia replied, unsure how much to reveal or what information to protect. "It's regarding the house."

"What house?" Jimmy asked.

Kate gave Amelia a sharp look, but it was too late. Megan had thrown her finger across the marina toward the cove. "*Our* house," she answered. "The one on the harbor."

***

Lunch was long over. Kate had excused herself to return to Michael, leaving Amelia and Megan to flounder about. Clara had given Amelia her house key so they could go back to her place—which they would do, at least for a while to let Dobi out and freshen up—but after that?

Wait for Kate to finish her super-secret-exclusive-executor-attorney meeting?

Apparently.

Jimmy trailed behind the two remaining women as they strolled slowly around the village, playing tourist and gossiping, a ritual of any tightly bonded sisters. Or even loosely bonded sisters.

Megan didn't bother to lower her voice when she began to ask about Amelia's relationship. "Construction worker? He looks more like a model. Acts like one, too," she remarked when they emerged from White Birch Soaps and Sundries.

Jimmy stepped out just after, and, having missed Megan's question, swooped in beside Amelia and slid an arm around her waist. "Ice cream anyone? I saw a place between the clothing boutique and the hair salon."

Megan twisted her lips into a knowing smirk, but Amelia wasn't sure if her judgment was for his use of the word "boutique" or his utter inability to read a situation.

Or, his ability to read a situation perfectly well and play it off like he was a dopey interloper.

"Sure, yeah," Amelia answered brightly. "Ice cream. Then we need to check on Dobi."

Jimmy flashed a grin. "You two go grab a couple of seats. I'll get us the good stuff. What's your poison, Megs?" he asked, shooting a finger gun at her.

To Amelia's surprise, her younger, ruthless sister recovered quickly from the unwelcome nickname, shaking her head and finally replying, "Vanilla bean on a waffle cone."

He nodded then aimed his finger to Amelia. "Babe?"

Amelia gave him a look. "You know my favorite."

He drew his hand to his mouth in a philosophical pose. "For my beautiful actress? Has to be... mint chocolate chip, which is also my favorite. Great minds think alike, right?"

"Oh my Lord," Megan murmured beside Amelia, and the latter swatted her sister's shoulder.

"Rocky road, please," Amelia said at last, tugging Megan in the opposite direction, toward a common area deck. Jimmy danced away with another goofy smile.

"You just can't help yourself but to be rude?" she snarled to Megan as they found a set of Adirondack chairs on the wooden platform that stretched out from the village.

"Amelia, be real. You two don't go together. What do you see in him?"

A long pause gave it away. "I think Kate likes him?" was all Amelia could respond with, at first. But she quickly added, "Clara says he's nice."

"They haven't had the chance to knock you upside the head, yet. I do. Dump that guy. Sooner rather than later. What is he even doing here, Amelia?"

She shrugged. "He's like a puppy dog. He's out of work but he's trying really hard to find something."

"None of that makes sense. He looks like he'd grab a screwdriver if you asked for a hammer. Don't you see any of this?"

Amelia nodded sadly. "Yes, I totally do. But, he's good to me. And he's so... *sexy*."

Megan recoiled. "Please never use that word again, first of all. Second of all, your standards are too low. I need to set you up with a quality person. That's your problem, Amelia. You don't know how to pick."

"I pick just fine, thank you."

"No. If you were a good picker, you'd be married with five kids, happily holed up in a three-bedroom in the suburbs of Detroit with someone like... like... I don't know. Like Michael Matuszewski. Instead, you have a chubby Weiner dog in a studio warehouse of an apartment in New York, where you wait tables and line up for auditions, accepting crappy roles when you could be making it big somewhere else. With *someone* else."

Amelia swallowed and turned her head to her sister. Tears welled in her eyes. "Are you seriously doing this right now?"

"Seriously doing what? Telling you what you need to hear? Yeah, I am."

Closing her eyes tightly, Amelia willed away the urge to cry before finding a smooth, calm answer. "You just told me to raise my standards. Now, you're saying I should drop everything and leave New York and take up a post as an unhappy housewife who's next in line for a divorce?" She had no idea where it came from. Amelia had never been good at snappy retorts. She'd make a terrible lawyer or sketch comedienne. Improv was not her area of expertise.

But there she was, shooting Megan's own admonitions right back at her.

Megan shifted in her chair, her voice softening. She didn't quite react to the brutal comeback, but there was a change in her tone. "Amelia, listen. Jimmy seems fun. And, he is handsome. Really handsome. Maybe he's good with his hands, too," she paused and lowered her chin, and Amelia couldn't suppress the childish grin that formed across her mouth. Megan went on, "Who knows? If the house needs a few repairs, he might just be our guy."

Amelia raised her eyes to Megan, listening carefully.

"I know you see my life and think that what I have is misery. Sometimes it is. I want a job. A passion. I want to lose Brian and get out from a boring marriage, sure. But," Megan blinked, and Amelia could have sworn she saw the reflection of a tear along her sister's lash line. "Just trust me on this, Amelia. I think you could do better."

"What about you?" Amelia replied. "Is that why you're divorcing Brian? Because you could do better? Because you could find some guy on your little dating app who ticks off one of the boxes that Brian doesn't?"

The tear found its way over the edge of Megan's kohl-lined lower eyelid and trailed down her cheek until she raised her hand and wiped it away. "I'm not looking for anyone," Megan spat back. Glancing over her shoulder. "I'm—"

"I think you need to reconsider the divorce."

There. Amelia had said it. The thing that had been on her mind since Megan revealed she was filing. The thing that had been on all their minds. It was a fool's move. Brian wasn't perfect, and neither was their marriage, no doubt.

But Megan seemed to be... searching. However, Amelia didn't entirely believe her younger sister was searching for a *new man*. Just a new chapter, maybe.

Megan frowned deeper and shook her head, anger pooling in her eyes.

But Amelia was on a roll. "You don't need a divorce, *Megs*," she said, her lips curling into a smile as she looked out over the marina at the house. *Their* house. "You need a *project*."

Chapter 11—Megan

Amelia didn't know squat about love or life. That much was clear.

But, Megan did like the idea of a project. A distraction. Something to pull her out of the rut she'd fallen into.

The house on the harbor *could* be that project. But it *wouldn't*. They were selling. Splitting it three ways (four if they contested effectively) and selling.

If she was honest with herself, Megan knew Nora's final wish was unfair. Clara deserved as much or more than the rest of them.

So then why was the poor thing excluded with such finality?

Megan knew the truth. They all knew the truth—except for Clara.

Maybe they could simply agree to give Clara The Bungalows? Maybe there was a better way to find a fair solution than rewriting Nora's last will and testament?

If the sisters had the chance to split the house three ways and keep even just two of the properties functioning as income, that'd leave enough money for Megan to move out on Brian, buy a whole *new* house, pay for Sarah's college tuition, *and* follow the secret dream she had. Opening her business. A small-town matchmaking enterprise. Maybe, she'd even do it in Birch Harbor.

But probably not.

Too close to her sisters.

Too close to their drama.

Jimmy returned with the ice cream, and Megan took her time working away at the chunky sweet edges while Amelia bit down through the top, her lips smacking around the cream loudly.

Megan laughed at the sight and sound.

"Sorry," Amelia said as she swallowed the massive bite. She held a hand over her lips to cover the mess. "Like Clara, I've been dieting off and on. I'm starving. Didn't you see? I had a spinach wrap. For God's sake, who substitutes spinach for bread? Me, I guess. I'm trying to lose ten for Lady Macbeth. But I can't resist sweets."

"Ten pounds in a week?"

Jimmy guffawed. "I know, right? She's perfect just the way she is."

As he said it, a group of college-aged girls in string bikinis trickled past toward the dock.

Megan watched in morbid fascination as Jimmy nearly dropped his cone onto the grass. He legitimately could not tear his eyes away from the grotesque scene of tanned butt cheeks peeking beneath bright bottoms and pointy shoulder blades wedged high and tight along slender backs.

She couldn't help it. Megan raised her hand and snapped her fingers in front of his face, more for her own benefit than Amelia's.

Jimmy raised his eyebrows and fumbled his hands, catching his ice cream cone flat on one palm, green sludge dripping faster than he could lick it away.

Megan shook her head, pointed her finger sternly at Amelia, and said, "I guess *you* already *have* a project."

Together, they burst out giggling as Jimmy apologized awkwardly and left, muttering some lame excuse about finding napkins.

***

After ice cream, Amelia had suggested that Jimmy head back to New York. Instead, he doubled down on his dumbery and said he'd wait it out at the motel.

"You might need my help this week," he offered weakly, his tail halfway between his legs by then.

"Even if we need you, we won't *want* you," Megan answered. Amelia stared daggers at her, but she didn't care. It had to be said. Jimmy, in all his sweet-talking, hot-stuff-walking glory, was a sleaze. And Megan would take a computer nerd over a sleaze any day of the week.

The whole scene had made her seriously, and painfully, reconsider everything she had ever known about her marriage. Especially about Brian's role in it. She began to question if Sarah was an ally or a victim, after all. If, maybe, awfully, Megan had poisoned her teenage daughter's brain, setting the stage for the girl to consider her own father a dope.

Megan's stomach started cramping as she reflected on it all.

Brian wasn't a dope. In fact, in his younger years, he'd rivaled Jimmy for good looks and toned abs. Sure, he'd hit middle age. But hadn't Megan, for that matter? Hadn't everyone?

But no matter that, she reminded herself, she hadn't entered into filing for a divorce lightly. It had come after years of neglect. Between them both. They were *both* to blame for a failed marriage. And who could fix a failed marriage?

***

Soon enough, the two sisters found themselves trudging back along Harbor Avenue toward The Bungalows. Jimmy had convinced Amelia to let him stay in town. They even had dinner plans. It was nauseating, but Megan had more important things to worry about.

The conversation about Clara and the house was on the tip of her tongue, but Amelia seemed distracted by her own problems.

Still, they were in Birch Harbor to handle Nora's aftermath. Or, rather, the aftermath of Nora.

"What do you think about the house?" Megan asked Amelia at last.

The older one turned to her just as they walked through the waist-high picket fence that ran along the front of the little complex.

"Do you mean the harbor one? Or the cottage, because I've been thinking about the cottage, too. I mean, is that where everything *is*? Or did Mom leave a lot at the house on the harbor?"

Megan shrugged. "I'm not sure. When we went to the cottage before the funeral, it seemed like everything was sort of... I don't know *in order*. Like she had made plans for an easy turnover. Like she was checking out of a hotel rather than dying."

Amelia paused when they reached Clara's unit. "I haven't been back to the harbor house in months. Clara's been the one keeping it up. She'd know better."

"Speaking of which," Megan answered, capitalizing. "Are we really going to split that place three ways? What about Clara? What do *you* think about the will?"

"I think it's awful, sure. But Kate is there now, reading some private paperwork. So maybe there's another heirloom for Clara, you know? Maybe Mom put together the will, then later added a letter that indicated Clara should actually keep The Bungalows or the cottage or the land. Or maybe there was cash left. Michael didn't tell us about her liquid assets, right?"

All good points, and all reasonable assumptions.

"If Mom left Clara out of the will, Amelia—" Megan went on, as Amelia thrust the brass key into the lock and turned it, spurring Dobi into a feverish barking barrage.

Amelia answered before Megan could finish. "We don't know what the letter says, Megan. Mom was kooky, but she wasn't evil. I'm positive she left *something* substantial for Clara, too."

"But what if she didn't?" Megan pressed.

Amelia scooped Dobi into her arms and attached a thin leash to the dog's collar before frowning at her younger sister. "Why *wouldn't* she?"

Megan crossed her arms. "You know *exactly* why."

Chapter 12—Clara

Clara unlocked the door at the end of her hallway, effectively sneaking in during the tail end of the lunch period.

Any moment now, stinky pubescent pre-teens and teenagers would be tumbling into the hall, lining up outside one of the four classrooms, anxious to collapse into a plastic desk chair where they would spend the next fifty-five minutes complaining, peeking at their phones, and generally doing anything other than learning.

It was Clara's burden to bring them back on board. One she relished. One she was good at. Her kids, as she called her students both affectionately and sometimes aggravatedly, had become her world. Even before her mother died, Clara wrapped up all of her hopes and dreams in her classes. Their test scores were her test scores. Their spelling errors were her spelling errors. Their engagement in the lesson was hers. And their bad moods were hers, too. It was a symbiotic relationship of the highest order.

They taught each other.

And today's lesson was going to fail everyone. Especially Clara.

She propped the heavy wooden door, the same one that the old school was built around in the early twentieth century, the one that sequestered her with hormonal seventh and eighth graders.

"Miss Hannigan?" a small voice echoed from the doorway as Clara tucked her handbag into the bottom drawer of the filing cabinet.

She turned on a sensible clog heel to see Mercy Hennings standing there, her hands clutching her backpack straps at the shoulders. Mercy Hennings was possibly the prettiest girl at Birch Harbor Secondary, even when compared against the makeup-faced seniors. And, surprisingly, Mercy was by far the kindest.

She was Clara's favorite, actually. Yes. Teachers had favorite students.

"Hi, Mercy," Clara answered. "Is everything okay?" They glanced up at the clock at the same time, budgeting how many minutes they had for whatever private conversation the girl was hoping to start.

"You weren't here this morning," Mercy pointed out.

Clara nodded. "I know. Did things go well with the sub? I had a family matter to handle."

The girl shrugged. "It went okay. I just wanted to pass in my homework to you instead of to the substitute."

Clara smiled. This was classic Mercy. Anxious. Worrisome. "Thanks, Mercy. I'll take it." She reached out as the girl handed over a neatly typed page.

After glancing at it, Clara frowned. "I think this is the wrong paper, sweetheart."

Mercy had given her a science report rather than the literature analysis she'd assigned the week before. The girl winced and began shuffling furiously through her backpack.

"Mercy, don't worry about it. You can bring it in tomorrow."

"No, no. I'll find it. I promise. I don't want to use my homework pass—"

Clara held up a hand. "You don't have to. Just bring it tomorrow. No problem, okay?"

But Mercy would not accept the exception, apologizing again before zipping her backpack in disappointment and muttering that she'd run home after school and bring it back by four o'clock.

Frowning and sighing, Clara again redirected her. "I won't be here, Mercy. I have some things going on that I have to see to after school."

The bell rang, and Mercy muttered a final apology then scurried off through the halls just before fifth period piled up by the doorway.

"Good afternoon!" Clara sang out as cheerfully as she could muster.

Typically, a day at work could distract Clara from bad news that seemed to take a regular hold on her personal life. She could sink her fears into Robert Frost or Edgar Allan Poe and find herself deep in the enchantment of bringing to life the old stuff for the new set of emerging readers. Emerging literarians, as she often called her students to their half-hearted scoffs.

But not today. All through her grammar lesson she kept stealing glances at her phone, waiting for a text from Kate. Some indication that the will was phony or wrong.

Anything.

But it never came.

Fifth hour slogged along. Then sixth. By seventh hour, Clara's planning period, she was ready to ask Mrs. Adamski if she could leave before the final bell.

She shuffled the papers on her desk into tidy piles, turned her computer off, and collected her handbag. Just as she opened the door to leave, her phone buzzed loudly.

Scrambling for it, Clara nearly missed the call. It was Kate.

"I don't have much news," her older sister admitted, as Clara hesitated to leave her classroom.

Feeling the threat of tears, Clara thought better of heading to the principal's office. Instead, she slid into a student desk and asked Kate to explain.

"Well," Kate started, "I talked to Michael, and he thinks we have a case for protesting the will."

"Protesting?"

"Right," Kate answered. Clara could hear traffic in the background. "You should have a claim. The fact that you were totally left out is unconscionable. Michael agreed, but... "

"But what?" Clara dropped her purse on the desk and stood, pacing now. A renewed energy coursed through her veins. Anger, probably. Anxiety, too.

"There's a complication," Kate said at last.

Clara shook her head. "What complication? That Mom was losing her mind? I fed her. I gave her sponge baths, Kate. I was there with her in the cottage every single day until the end. How could she do this?"

Kate's voice shook as she replied, "Mom wasn't well. But, that's not the complication, Clara."

"Then what is the complication?"

A pause filled their phone call, and a million things ran through Clara's mind. The unfairness. The bizarreness.

Something did *not* add up.

Especially when Kate said, "Just, you know. Something funky. A complication. Clara, I have to go. Let's get together later tonight. We'll talk it through, okay?"

But Clara didn't have a chance to agree. Kate had already hung up.

Chapter 13—Kate

Kate slid into her car and pressed her fingers to her throbbing temples. She had two choices. Read the letter now, or read it with Amelia and Megan, people who knew the truth and could support her if the letter was upsetting.

But that was just the issue. What was *in* the letter? Was it something she'd prefer to keep private?

Who knew?

She'd share it with Amelia and Megan. They'd figure everything out together and *then* bring Clara in. They'd fight the will, the properties *and* the furniture and heirlooms inside of the properties would be split evenly, and they'd all move on. Back to normal.

Kate would find an affordable, smaller house. Maybe closer to the boys. Clara would keep teaching and carry on as Birch Harbor's pretty hermit. Maybe, Clara would even take on the family membership plan at the Country Club and start hosting stilted dinner affairs where she flitted from catered table to catered table.

Doubtful, but at least Clara could start to love her life for once.

Amelia would land an acting gig and never talk to them again once she found that fame she'd been searching for. And Megan would get a divorce and stay put in her three-bedroom two-story in the suburbs, doing whatever it was she did with her free time. Scrolling through her phone with a permanent scowl, probably.

With the plan firmly in mind, Kate dialed Amelia and threw her car into reverse.

Her sister answered on the first ring. "Hey, how'd it go?"

Kate replied quickly, her breath shallow. "Meet me at the house on the harbor. I'm on my way there now. Bring Megan."

***

Kate stood on the street side of the house. Harbor Avenue stretched like an artery from the south side of the marina up through to the village, but it forked off into something of a frontage road, offering private access to the strip of homes that dotted the lake.

Each of the houses along that narrow side street was immaculately maintained. The Hannigan home, however, less so. Clara had done all she could, no doubt, but she—unlike the couples and families who summered in Birch Harbor—didn't quite have the motivation or even the means to hire a landscaper or a handyman to come and regularly help with upkeep. Plus, Nora had refused to budget for it.

In Nora's years of tending to various rental properties, she relied, as she often said in a put-on Blanche DuBois drawl, *on the kindness of strangers*.

That wasn't entirely true, since there were few strangers among those who lived in Birch Harbor year-round. However, Nora was a woman who got her way.

A sweet smile to the custodian at Birch Harbor Secondary set her up with an emergency contact for water leaks or power outages.

The right compliment to the groundskeeper at the Country Club resulted in a lifetime of monthly hedge trims and brush-and-bulky hauls.

As for nearly everything else, well, Nora had figured it out herself. Applying her father's knowledge and her mother's intellect, she came to be able to fight her way to fix or update anything all by herself. No hired man necessary. Just a second trip to the salon to touch up her manicure.

Still, it was curious that, when Nora decided she was abandoning the big house for her creek-side cottage, she also abandoned her hard work there. And with that, the helpful friends who no longer found their paycheck in the enigmatic smile and home-baked goods of their patroness. Those gentlemen, who'd aged along with Nora, found other ways to spend their time.

Unsurprisingly, Nora allowed her daughters to pick up the slack, much of which fell to Clara. She grew tired of it, or so was Kate's observation of the matter. But it was an observation she refused to share, since she wasn't helping much herself.

But, Kate helped in another way. She managed The Bungalows, offering robust contracts that stipulated far-reaching responsibilities of the tenants. But even that was growing tenuous.

Soon, she'd need a real property manager, someone who could make the bigger repairs that Kate had begun to pay out of pocket years earlier. Mentally, she added that task to her to-do list: find a handyman tenant who would take care of the place better than Clara, who didn't grow up the same as her older sisters or mother, with the expectation of corralling the troops for a weekend of scraping hard water off of swamp cooler panels.

Presently, Kate stood on the sidewalk, just inches from a short, white picket fence, the same style Nora had erected at The Bungalows. Beyond the fence glowed a thick, shaggy green lawn, in desperate need of a mow. Bushes and flowers grew wild along the terraces that crisscrossed prettily beneath the front porch. And behind the untamed yard loomed the house. Two stories. Three if one counted the attic. Four, even, if one counted the basement, which Kate always had as a child.

Back then, growing up and even well after her college years, Kate took great pride in living in that house. She and her sisters pitched in the year their mother decided to paint it a warm, rich red. It took them all summer just to get the front of the first floor coated once. That was when Nora agreed to hire out. A rare occurrence, indeed.

As the years wore on, Kate became aware of flaws and attributes that weren't previously apparent.

The red paint had long begun to peel and, in some places, curl up and chip off.

The weathered shutters had presented shabby chic potential, but they now threatened to pull away from their hinges. Kate imagined them breaking loose and sailing out to the lake like miniature wooden barges on a waveless sea.

She unlatched the squat fence gate and stepped across the invisible line that divided Birch Harbor from the old Hannigan family home and its previous inhabitants.

As Kate neared the house, she noticed one quality that had been nagging her lately—just how close the property was to the harbor. Less than a stone's throw to Birch Village and the marina.

Without a doubt, it would sell. It would sell, and Kate and her sisters would get everything in order. Between proceeds from the sale and income from the investment properties, as long as they could agree to split things fairly, Kate saw a future in which she could, for once, have some peace. No worrying about bills. Not her mom's. Not her own.

"Get off my lawn!"

Kate spun on a heel, her face flushing and her pulse tripling in the time it took her to locate the person yelling at her.

Her eyes bobbed wildly before landing on two women, walking in long strides from up the sidewalk.

Megan and Amelia.

The latter waved her arm in a wide half circle. "I said get off my lawn!" she hollered again, her voice deep, disguised. Megan laughed beside her, and Kate smiled at last.

"You scared me," she called back. "Sounds like your voice lessons are paying off, though. That's a good baritone."

Amelia recovered from her own laughter. "I haven't taken voice in years. I gave up any chance of musicals long ago."

Kate walked back to the gate and opened it for them, and they gathered together on the lawn, examining the house again.

Megan sighed. "What has Clara been *doing* all this time?"

Defensiveness wrapped around Kate like a blanket, seizing her in paralysis for a moment before she answered honestly, deflated. "The bare minimum. It's all she *can* do, really."

Amelia and Megan glanced at each other, frowning in tandem. But Kate just shrugged, adding, "We haven't been here to help."

"She could have hired someone. Mom had an income stream, right?"

"A *limited* income stream," Kate answered.

"What do you mean 'limited?'" Megan pressed, crossing her arms over her chest. "The Bungalows are fully rented. Clara aside, we should be pulling in good money from three tenants, right?"

"Yes and no," Kate admitted. "Three tenants, yes. Two of them are long term people. They signed a contract back in the nineties, if you can believe that. They aren't paying much, and Mom never raised their rent. The third pays something more reasonable, but it's still not much. And I have to use some of that income to cover maintenance. Clara dips into whatever is left over to pay electric, gas, and water here." Kate waved a hand at the house. "And, we pay utilities for the cottage. And taxes on all four properties, the land included."

"You mean that farmland out west?" Amelia asked.

Kate nodded.

"It's exactly why we need to be smart about how we handle this. If we play our cards right and make good decisions, we will come out ahead, I promise," Kate pleaded to her sisters' impassive faces.

But they weren't having it. Megan cleared her throat. "So what about Clara? Why isn't she here?"

Chapter 14—Amelia

Amelia didn't quite share Megan's harsh agitation over how well—or how poorly—Clara had kept the place. Amelia understood Clara was just getting by. Each of them, after all, was just getting by. Megan with her divorce. Kate with her widowhood. And she, herself, with her wreck of a life.

Following Kate and Megan up to the porch, Amelia took in the place, admiring its stateliness and wondering, selfishly, if they might not make a buck. Something to help cover New York rent. Something to pay for a little Botox. *Something,* Amelia thought, to help her make more of her life than the depressing audition-rejection-waitressing cycle she'd found herself caught inside of like a hamster in a plastic wheel.

She watched as Kate pushed the spare key into the heavy brass key plate, turning the tarnished key and the knob below in tandem. But it didn't budge. She pushed the key farther to the left, then tried the knob again, rattling it. It gave a little, but Kate had to press her shoulder into the door to jostle the wood free. Amelia winced. She hadn't been back to the house in long enough that she felt like all three of them were trespassing somehow.

With one quick pop, Kate fell into the foyer, and a thick warmth sucked Amelia and Megan in behind her.

The air of the house hung still.

Amelia shut the door behind them by pushing her back against it.

Just across from the entryway unfurled the wide wooden staircase, rolling up to the second story landing like an architectural centerpiece. Ample floor space spread around it, original hardwood floors tracking back toward the kitchen, right toward the front hall—as their mother called it—and left toward the parlor.

Amelia took a tentative step into the front hall. Every piece of furniture was covered in heavy white sheets. An outline of a piano and that of a set of sofas confirmed that, actually, nothing much had changed other than a few years' worth of age settling into the room.

She turned and joined Megan and Kate, who began their tour in the opposite direction, through the parlor. Similarly, there, the sitting chairs and side tables stood draped. Dust had been slow to collect on top of the fabric, but Megan ran her finger along one cloth and held it up to reveal a gray oval.

Kate bit her lip. Megan dipped her chin to Amelia.

They moved into the kitchen. It was there that it occurred to Amelia how valuable the house just may be.

Rustic wooden countertops cut utilitarian angles around an ample island. Beneath the window, the porcelain farmhouse sink, complete with an apron, presented itself like a solitaire popping up from a thick, corroding gold band.

The fridge, a narrow, white piece from the mid-nineties, was the exact same one Amelia had used when she lived there. From it, she'd fetch milk for cereal in the mornings and a glass tray of butter for dinner rolls each night.

The kitchen table waited beneath yet another heavy tent. Consenting to an urge that tugged at her from the moment she saw all the drop cloths, Amelia gripped the edges of the one on the table and tugged hard, flourishing the fabric back like a matador.

The dust turned to an aerosol, blasting all three of their faces and tickling their throats into coughing fits.

"Gee, thanks, Amelia," Megan choked out at the end of a final wheeze.

"Don't be so dramatic," Amelia replied, grinning, and wiped her hands along her jeans. "I had to do it. The temptation was too strong."

Beneath the sheet was the same farmhouse-style table they'd used as children. It was an heirloom, from the Hannigan ancestors. One of many, to be sure.

The sisters stared at the wooden piece before moving on through the pantry and into a small dining room, one they'd never used with any regularity.

From there, they looped back to the staircase and split off. Kate and Amelia turned up the stairs, and Megan walked past, to the basement door which opened just between the kitchen and the foyer at the backside of the staircase.

As they explored, Amelia and Kate murmured remembrances about years gone past. Sliding down the banister and nearly cracking their heads open. Helping their mom strip, buff, stain, and wax the hardwood by hand, one room at a time. For as much work as they had all put into the house, it now felt like a waste.

Amelia broke away from Kate at the second landing and opted to take the narrow staircase at the far end of the hall, up to the attic.

It had been her space, as a child. A space where she put on her puppet shows and rehearsed for dance recitals—the dance recitals she presented for her mother and whatever friends were visiting for the evening.

When she made it up the stairs and through the narrow door, she came to a stop, unable to move beyond the few feet just inside the door. Towers of boxes blocked her access. Stacked in dense rows across the attic floor, they were entirely unfamiliar.

Pushing out a sigh, she turned and descended, rejoining Kate in the hallway.

Kate offered a weak smile. "Sheets everywhere. Otherwise, it's the same. Frozen in time, I guess."

Amelia nodded. "Let's find Megan."

***

They sat at the kitchen table; their three handbags propped by their feet. Megan picked at her chipping nail polish. Amelia flicked a glance to Kate, who held an envelope on top of the table, squarely in front of her.

Amelia shifted in her seat. "Wow," she began, attempting to break the ice. "A private document for the executor, or a private letter for *you*." She lifted an eyebrow and pretended to scrutinize her older sister. The effect seemed to agitate Kate, and Amelia laughed lightly. "I'm kidding. But what's inside?"

"And why is it a secret?" Megan added, dropping her hands to her lap. "And why isn't Clara here?"

Kate looked up at them, and Amelia thought she saw a tear form in her eye. But it was gone in a flash as the woman launched into what could only be called an appeal.

"First of all, I'm not inviting Clara to join us until we come to an agreement. I haven't opened this letter yet, and I'm not going to just yet. Regardless of what's inside, we have to make a decision about what we're going to do. And it has to be the *right* decision."

Amelia leaned back, taking in Megan's initial reaction. She tugged either side of her black hair behind her ears and looked back at Amelia, who shrugged.

"Go on," Amelia answered, propping her elbows on the table.

Kate licked her lips. "Clara belongs in the will."

Amelia sucked in a breath. "Well, obviously."

Megan cut in. "So then why isn't she?"

"We know why she isn't," Kate hissed.

"Because Mom was a mean old woman?" Megan replied.

Amelia shook her head and held her hands up in sharp angles. "No name-calling. No bitchiness." She felt the others narrow their eyes on her, so she went on. "Fact: Clara was left *nothing*. Fact: Clara should have gotten *something*."

"Fact," Megan inserted herself, her tone one of mockery, "it doesn't matter who was in the will if Kate is right about all these *bills*." The last word rolled off her tongue like poison.

"Okay, calm down," Kate answered. "I am *right* about the bills. But that doesn't change that we each get a piece of the pie. And it shouldn't change the fact that Mom made a mistake. We can fight this. We have to fight this for Clara. She doesn't deserve to be left out."

Amelia's face softened. She agreed with Kate. Clara deserved one-fourth. Each of them deserved exactly one-fourth. No matter their history.

"So can we agree to fight it?" Kate pressed. "Can we agree to contest the will on the grounds that Mom made an error?"

Amelia nodded right away.

Megan shrugged. "Sure. Yeah. Obviously it's not fair. Go ahead. Contest it. She's our *sister*, right?"

Kate frowned deeply. "Thank you. And anyway, maybe this letter explains things. If the house was not designated for one of us, then we'll have to share it anyway. I still don't think that's fair enough, though. Regardless I'll go back to Michael's office first thing in the morning and file an appeal."

"For the love of all that is good in this world, *open* the *letter*," Amelia demanded, softly pounding her fist on the top of the table.

Kate opened her mouth to reply, but she was thwarted by a deep, intrusive chime.

The doorbell.

Chapter 15—Megan

Megan strode to the front of the house in a huff, convinced it was a local busybody snooping for some sort of belated gossip.

She was wrong.

"Oh," she murmured, after tugging the door hard enough to nearly pull a muscle in her shoulder. "Hi."

Matt Fiorillo stood haplessly on the porch. He was dressed like he was about to go golfing—at a par 3 out in the sticks. A frumpy polo, untucked, above the most casual of khaki shorts. Ankle socks and clean white sneakers gave way to tanned, muscular legs.

He raised a hand and scratched his dark hair as he met Megan's gaze. "Megan?" he asked.

Megan had always liked Matt. Even after he and her sister broke up. She'd liked him in the way a girl admires a handsome distant relative. Perhaps, an uncle by marriage or a second cousin, twice removed—with fascination and a dose of envy.

If she was honest, Megan used Matt as a template, of sorts. He was the type of guy she wanted to marry. She'd always said that to herself.

And, in many ways, she was successful. Brian, too, was something of a puppy-dog type. Friendly and frumpy. Kind eyes. Gentle words. Brian, however, was more of an intellectual, preferring computers over cars and phone apps over fixer-uppers.

Of all the people in Birch Harbor who Megan had ever heard gossip about, Matt was not among them. Nor were any of the Fiorillos, really. It was a nice family. A lovable one.

"Matt? What are you doing here?" Megan glanced behind her, waiting for Kate and Amelia to appear at any moment.

He dropped his hand from his hair and tucked it into his front pocket. A deep sadness took hold of his face. "Megan, I'm so sorry to hear about your mom. I was at the funeral, but—"

"We were busy," Megan replied on his behalf. "It's okay. Thank you for coming, though."

Just then, Megan felt the air change behind her. Matt's eyes lifted.

She turned. Kate and Amelia stood there, both sets of their eyes frozen on him.

"Matt. Hi." The voice belonged to Kate, but Megan didn't recognize it. Her words came out pinched and high.

Megan cleared her throat and stepped aside. "Amelia, let's go to the parlor and leave these two alone."

Kate shook her head and pinned Megan with a look before glancing back to Matt. "No, no. It's fine. Matt, come in."

He thanked them and followed as Kate escorted everyone to the back porch, which was hitherto uncharted territory.

Megan was glad for the change of scenery, but even more, she was glad to be in on this little reunion, of sorts.

Things had not ended well with Kate and Matt. Megan was only in grade school when it happened, but she could remember the whole fiasco like the back of her hand. Kate's sobs. Matt's angry helplessness.

They'd both put up a good fight. One they thought no one had borne witness to.

But Megan had.

Twelve-year-olds were good at that sort of thing. Sneaking around and eavesdropping on their older sisters. Especially when a boy was involved.

But then, that memory extended far past the emotional night that pushed Matt away indefinitely.

That was the summer they went on *vacation*. All of them. Like a happy family. Their aunt's house in Arizona. Far away from Michigan. Far away from everyone.

The walk to the backyard felt long. Megan had flashbacks to when they lived there, Amelia and Kate always striding ahead of her and Megan doing her best to catch up. She didn't like to miss anything. And, usually, she didn't have to.

However, now was not a good time to meddle. Standing and facing the lake added to the discomfort Megan sensed. Amelia must have felt it, too, because she tugged Megan's arm lightly. "Come on. You were right. Why don't we let these two catch up? You and I can walk the grounds. I haven't been down to the lake in forever."

Megan, again, felt Kate's eyes bore a hole, but Matt smiled easily.

"Ten minutes," Kate called after Megan and Amelia. "Just give us ten minutes."

Amelia chuckled once they were on the far side of the lawn, stepping through the white wooden gate of the seawall and down to the little beach.

"What's funny?" Megan asked.

As if guided by muscle memory, they both kicked their shoes off and stepped into the warm sand. It curled up between Megan's toes, and she realized how much she missed it. The last time she'd sat out on the lake was years prior. Even then, when she had found herself on the shore, she hadn't taken her shoes off. She hadn't felt the sand on the bottom of her feet or sliding overtop. If she closed her eyes now, she could transport herself to Rehoboth or La Jolla.

Or, even better, she could transport herself to her childhood.

"This whole thing," Amelia spread her arms out wide and twirled in a circle. "Being home. Like, *home*, home. Mom. The weird-as-hell will. Matt," she lifted her chin up toward the porch. They were far enough away to be out of earshot, but Megan only stole a quick look.

"It's not that funny," Megan pointed out.

"Oh, it's funny. Life is funny, Megan."

They walked to the shoreline. Directly back from the property, a wide thatch of grass halted at the seawall. From there, lay a pristine sandy beach. But just yards off, in the direction of the harbor, spread a rocky outcropping. Though the waves of Lake Huron weren't the crashing kind, every so often a boat would zoom past and push water up against the rocks. The resulting splash turned the cove and the marina beyond into more than a community by the lake; Birch Harbor became a small town *on the water*.

Megan stared out and up the shore, beyond the marina. Miles north, past the tourist fanfare, stood one of Lake Huron's many lighthouses. Thoughts of her father and his parents washed over her—the grandparents that the Hannigan girls cuddled with, the ones who took them to the Detroit Zoo and the county fair. The ones who maintained the rickety old tower and the house beneath. She wondered who was running it currently. It still worked, after all.

"Why are you with Jimmy, Amelia?" It fell out of Megan's mouth before she could swallow it back. Megan felt now was the time to nail it down. She knew her sister deserved better than Jimmy, but she needed *Amelia* to see it, too. For her own good.

By the seawall at the far corner of the property there sat a small wooden shed, its boards dead and gray.

Amelia pointed to it. "Let's grab chairs and sit. They might be longer than ten minutes."

Soon enough, the two middle sisters were sitting with their feet in the water, idly lifting the shore on their toes and splashing it gently back out to the lake.

"Jimmy is… " Amelia began with a sigh.

Megan felt compelled to finish her sentence, but she refrained, trying to accept that it was far better for Amelia to find the truth on her own than for anyone else to thrust it at her.

After a beat, Amelia lifted her hands and slapped them back down on the arms of the chair. Megan winced. "Don't get a splinter." The wood of the chairs was sun-bleached and brittle.

A rumble of laughter caught in Amelia's throat and spread across to Megan. They giggled together. It felt good.

"Jimmy is your boyfriend," Megan said, her tone impartial as could be.

"Jimmy is my boyfriend, yes." Amelia stopped for a minute and furrowed her eyebrows. "Wow. Boyfriend. Am I fifteen?"

Again, they laughed, but this time it wasn't as light.

Megan kept quiet and picked at her nail polish. Little black flakes lifted up and carried off on the breeze. She glanced back toward the house. Kate and Matt weren't standing there anymore. Maybe they'd gone in.

"What do you think they're talking about?" Amelia asked.

Megan shrugged. "I doubt much. Kate isn't going to rehash the past. She's too focused on what's happening with the will."

"Clara deserves more," Amelia answered, her voice flattening. "You know that, right, Megan?"

Megan frowned. "Yes, I know that. But something doesn't add up."

Amelia didn't answer. Instead, she changed the conversation. "Have you talked to Brian since you've been here?"

Another breeze, a stronger breeze, whipped across their faces. Though it was getting later, and the air was turning cooler, the sun still hung in the sky behind them, casting their shadows onto the water. Megan stood abruptly and kicked water at hers, but it reappeared quickly, like a long, lifeless blob. Not quite a reflection. Still, it was her own image, stretching out into the lake from her feet, indelibly attached. "No," she answered.

"Does he know you're on that app?"

Megan turned sharply to her sister and narrowed her eyes. "I'm not on the app. I mean I'm on it, but—it's not what you think," she replied. Her breath turned sour and her mouth grew dry. It was an internal struggle that she should be able to share with Amelia. With anyone, really. But she was too scared things might not pan out. She was scared it was a dead end. And then she'd look the fool.

"It's not what I think? Then tell me, what should I think?" Amelia replied. Her voice was soft, but her words pushed Megan to the brink of revealing her little secret.

No. Another week or two. Then things might materialize. She might be able to share. It might be different. And anyway, they weren't together in Birch Harbor for Amelia or anyone else to pick apart Megan's life decisions. "I'm getting a *divorce*. And, actually, the dating app has nothing to do with it," she spat back.

But as she walked away from Amelia and back toward the house, Megan felt a knot form in her throat. She couldn't swallow past it. It stayed there, thickening, until she began to wonder if her plan was a joke. Who was Megan Stevenson to pursue her dreams?

As she crossed through the gate and up the sidewalk, Megan's phone vibrated in her back pocket.

For the first time in forever, she hoped it was him.

Not any of the men whose in-app messages she'd always ignored.

She hoped it was *him*. Hers.

Brian.

But it wasn't.

Chapter 16—Kate

Kate hadn't spoken to Matt Fiorillo in years. Even at the funeral, they successfully avoided each other. At the time, his presence had even felt... voyeuristic.

"Why'd you come, Matt?" she asked as he followed her through to the kitchen, where she landed behind a chair. She felt a little naked in front of him. She hadn't brought her most fashionable outfits or all of her makeup and hair products. He was seeing her plainly, as she was.

"Mainly to see if you are okay."

"Really?" She frowned. Kate had no reason to be angry with Matt. And, she wasn't. But still, she couldn't quite trust him, interrupting her and her sisters like that.

He dropped his voice. "Really. Are you?"

"Am I what?"

"Are you okay?"

Her eyes fell to his hands, work worn and bigger than she remembered. "I guess."

In a moment, he was next to her. "Is there anything I can do?"

Shaking her head, Kate blinked away a tear. She wanted to ask him about himself, but it wasn't the time. Maybe it never would be.

"I'm here for you. Whatever you need. I can run errands. I can give you money—whatever you need."

She looked up at him. "We don't need your help, Matt. Thanks, but we will be okay."

"And," he replied, pausing momentarily. "Your *sisters*? How are they?"

Kate looked up sharply. "Fine. They're fine. There are some complications, but we'll make it work."

He inhaled deeply and took a step back before waving his hand around. "What are you doing with this place?"

A shrug was all Kate could offer in reply. "We don't know. My mom wasn't very clear, unfortunately. Or, if she was, then we haven't found out yet."

"It is staying in the family, right? You four will get it, though?"

She frowned. "I hope so."

Matt stepped back toward her, tucked the edge of his fingers under her chin and said, "Please let me know if I can *help*. Do you promise, Kate?"

A single tear spilled over her lash line and onto his hand. Kate sniffled and pulled away. "Of course. Thanks." He started to walk out, but Kate called after him. "Matt."

"Yes?"

"If, for some reason, we can't keep this place—" she started.

He cut her off. "I'll buy it. Name your price, and I'll buy it."

Chapter 17—Clara

"Megan?"

Her sister answered the phone just before Clara suspected she was about to be hit with a voicemail greeting.

"Hey, Clara," Megan replied. She sounded tired. Deflated. Disappointed, even?

"Where are you? Where are Kate and Amelia?"

"We're here. At the house."

Clara was about to untuck herself from her car, but waited instead. "You mean the Heirloom house?"

"Yep," Megan answered.

Muffled barks floated through the walls of her unit down to her parking space at The Bungalows. Clara had always wanted a dog. But not a dog like Dobi, insecure and anxious. Always barking. Always wondering where Amelia was, no doubt.

Dobi was like a sweeter and more neurotic version of Trudy, Nora's late Chihuahua. Trudy, the demon pup, as Clara had nicknamed her. The white miniature beast hated everyone except Nora. It was definitely for the best that the poor thing preceded her mistress in death, because Trudy would have been the one remnant of her mother's estate that no one would fight for. Then again, that wasn't true. In reality, Clara would have accepted Trudy with open arms. She'd be like a little version of Nora, terrorizing the town by day and stealing table scraps at night. Though, unlike Nora, Trudy didn't mind an extra pound here or there.

Clara forced an errant sob back down her throat.

She wasn't sure what her next move ought to be. Ask to talk to Kate and rip into her for hanging up? Pretend nothing was happening and just show up at the house. *Surprise! Face me! Face the one who was left out of the will!*

Instead, she closed her eyes and leaned into her seat back, waiting.

Megan murmured something to someone in the background, and Clara could have sworn she'd overheard a man's voice. "Who's that?" she asked, her eyes shut in the still, warm air of her car.

Her sister came back on the line. "Matt Fiorillo. He came by to ask about the house, actually."

"What?" Clara's eyes shot open. "What do you mean he asked about the house?"

"He wants to put an offer in, I guess. He and Kate chatted for a while and—"

Megan's voice was cut in half, and then Kate's replaced it. "Clara?"

Clara scowled. "You hung up on me."

"Listen, I'm sorry. Why don't you come over here, okay? To the Harbor Avenue house."

"Fine," Clara snapped, tapping her phone off. She was about to start the engine again but guilt nagged at her, and she went inside, clipped Dobi's leash to his collar, and led him to the courtyard instead. It was a break for both of them and a moment for Clara to compose her thoughts and think about what it was she really wanted.

Because the time had come for her to ask for it.

***

"He said he'd make an offer." Kate avoided Clara's gaze.

"*That's* why he came over?" Amelia asked, her eyes bulging. "He didn't want to, like, *talk*?"

Clara watched as Amelia and Kate exchanged an unreadable expression.

"You called me over to tell me someone wants to buy the house? Are you also going to clue me in on the secret?" Clara stood in the doorway to the kitchen as her sisters sat at the table. Only Kate offered her a supplicating look.

"What secret?" Megan asked. "There is no secret. Mom left you out of the will because she was losing it."

"Megan," Kate hissed.

"It's as much as we know, actually." Amelia straightened in her seat and ran her hands down her thighs.

Evening had set over Birch Harbor, and the lake outside the kitchen windows glimmered in the backdrop.

Clara's stomach started cramping. "So, then what's the plan?" she asked at last, her hands clasped tightly below her waist.

"The plan is this," Kate answered. As she spoke, Clara detected a delicacy in her words. A hesitancy, even. "We are going—well, *I* am going to Michael Matuszewski's office first thing in the morning and filing an appeal."

A heavy sigh filled Clara's mouth and she pushed it out, nodding in agreement. "That's great." Her hands relaxed and she shoved each into her back pockets and leaned against the doorframe.

"And," Kate went on, "once we get that in place, we'll talk to Matt again. See if he's serious and if he can make a reasonable offer."

"What about the other properties?" Clara asked, drawing a fingernail to her lips and chewing distractedly. "And are we *positive* we want to sell?"

It was Megan who answered this time. She spoke softly, warmly even. It was a breath of fresh air after what felt like ages of attitude, like a flip had switched. "Hopefully, Clara, the appeal will result in an even split. I think our goal is one of two things, and that's why you're here."

Lifting an eyebrow, Clara studied each of her sisters in turn. They seemed... sad. Anxious.

"Okay?" Clara asked, feeling all of her youth at that moment. Familiar anxiety bobbed at the surface of her mind, and she thought back to Mercy Hennings. Sweet Mercy who made a special trip to turn in her paper, on the brink of tears, praying to not get marked down. On her way out, Clara had all but bumped head on into Mercy's dad as he was searching for the front door of the building. When Clara asked him if he was dropping something off, he must have realized she suspected his delivery was meant for her.

They exchanged a quick introduction, and Clara apologized that she couldn't chat longer, promising him an extended conference at the end of the school year. He'd thanked her profusely, and she'd felt gratified to be in the presence of a supportive parent. In fact, the whole thing had been the highlight of her day.

"We have a proposal." Amelia cut into Clara's reverie, and she snapped out of it, listening now with acute focus. Amelia looked at Kate, who took over.

"Originally, it appeared that we'd have to liquidate in order to split everything evenly and adhere to the demands of the estate. That, or rent out and split the income. The second option would allow you to stay on at The Bungalows."

"Right," Clara interjected, unsure if she was following as well as she ought to be.

"But that's our question for you, Clara," Megan said. "Do you want to stay on at The Bungalows? Where do you see yourself?"

Clara frowned. She'd never once considered leaving her little one-bedroom by the Birch Harbor Bridge. It was a central location, and it was... actually, no. It wasn't quite home. She opened her mouth, about to claim that she'd love to have the house. The one in which they currently met.

But that wasn't true either.

Clara felt a disconnect from the house on the harbor. She tolerated life in Unit 2. Being relatively asocial and particularly disinterested in the regular maintenance and management that her position as property manager demanded, Clara realized she'd been living someone else's life for a while.

A long while.

She'd been living the life Nora had assigned her to. Keeper of her mother. Middleman to her out-of-town sisters. Single, youthful spinster whose only real escape was *work*, of all things.

"I don't want The Bungalows. And I don't want this place either," she answered, startling herself as much as the others.

"So what do you want, Clara?" Kate asked, cocking her head.

Clara swallowed and furrowed her brows as she stared off into the inky lake in the distance, the lake she swam alone in as a girl. The lake that boasted loud tourists on their weekender Jet Skis.

She thought of school and her students. The pile of papers to be graded each night. The literature-rich lessons she'd pored over every weekend.

Mostly, she thought of her last days with their mother and the quiet time they shared, the private moments. Tending to Nora alone was hard. But it was an experience Clara wouldn't give up—even if she had known what she knew now, about the will. And yet, it never provided the insight that they now desperately needed to solve the puzzle. Spending day after day at the cottage—night after night for weeks and then months had resulted in nothing but exhaustion. And now, confusion.

Mustering the energy to reply, Clara gave her sisters the truth. "I have no idea what I want."

Chapter 18—Kate

There was no returning home. Not until the estate was settled and a firm plan was in place. And, although Kate could have either stayed at the house on the harbor *or* the cottage, she chose to bunk up with Megan on the pull-out sofa in Clara's bungalow.

It was like a sleepover, and the meeting they'd had the night before softened the hardship of an extended stay in town. Then again, Kate had to admit that being back in Birch Harbor was more good than bad.

They'd wrapped up their meeting at the house and stopped by Fiorillo's for a glass of wine. Clara had asked about Matt's connection to the restaurant, which prompted Kate, Amelia, and Megan to question the girl's knowledge of her own town.

Unwilling to discuss Matt Fiorillo one second longer, she'd batted away the topic, explaining to Clara that the owners were his folks. End of story. Nothing to see there.

Now, they were all tucked into their respective beds, Dobi whipping through the house like a maniac as Amelia and Clara giggled in the back bedroom like little girls.

"See what I have to put up with?" Megan asked Kate once the lights were out.

Kate nodded in the darkness and turned to face her sister. "Do you miss her?" she whispered to Megan, feeling sad all of a sudden.

"Who? Mom?"

"Yeah." Kate tried to focus on Megan's face, tried to assess her reaction. Her features. Her expression. But it was too dark.

Megan was lying on her back, staring straight ahead, unmoving, as far as Kate could tell.

"Yeah. Of course. Just because things got bad at the end doesn't mean I don't miss her. She's our mom. I love her. Loved her. *Love* her. Jeez. How do you talk about someone who's dead, Katie?"

Kate smiled at the nickname. No one had called her Katie in years. Decades. "I know." She let out a sigh and shifted under the covers, mirroring Megan and facing the ceiling. The shape of a modest ceiling fan whirred above, blowing Kate's hair in ticklish wisps across her forehead. She hunkered down deeper in the covers.

"Do you miss her?"

Kate blinked at the question. "Mom? Of course."

"Yeah, but... your relationship was... different. We all know that. At least, Amelia and I do."

Considering this, Kate hesitated before answering. No matter what she said in response, she would never come close to articulating her real feelings, which were as complicated as the estate itself. And even if she offered a decent response, it would result in a lifting of the floodgates. Memories from the hardest years would pour out, and Kate would get no sleep.

"I loved Mom. Always will." It was a simple answer. It should have been enough to end the conversation that Kate regretted ever opening. But it wasn't, and Megan pressed on.

"Did you open the letter yet?"

Kate shook her head and pushed her tongue to the roof of her mouth hard, willing away the tears that had climbed up the back of her throat.

Moments passed, and the tongue trick didn't work. She gave in to quiet crying and pressed the heels of her hands as deep into her eyes as she could bear.

The bed creaked and dipped beneath Kate's body, and she nearly fell into the middle toward Megan, who was wiggling closer. "It's okay," Megan whispered, slipping her arms around Kate and squeezing her shaking, sobbing body close. "It's okay, sis."

***

Megan had fallen asleep somewhere around ten or eleven. Kate waited until two in the morning until she gave up on any shut-eye and snuck out of bed and to her purse.

She wasn't quite sure what she was waiting for. A moment alone? A chance to breathe? Or, most likely, courage?

As Kate pulled the envelope from her purse, her heart pounded in her chest. Her mom could have said anything. It could be an apology. It could be a chastisement. It could be nothing, even. After all, in the past couple months, Nora's downward spiral knew no bounds. She might have repackaged her electric bill, for all Kate knew.

She glanced back to ensure Megan was still asleep, then stole away through the backdoor and onto the quaint porch. There, propping her phone like a flashlight, she studied the white envelope, trying to make sense of the past day.

But she came up empty.

Quietly and delicately, Kate slid a finger beneath the far corner of the sealed flap, tugging the glue free in a smooth drag.

The letter was not, actually, a letter.

It was not an electric bill, either.

It was the torn page of a notebook or journal of some sort—unlined, beige, its edge revealing a hasty rip rather than a clean tear.

Kate frowned, her eyes dancing back and forth to make sense of what it was Nora had seen fit to leave.

But there was no puzzle in the handwriting. No evidence of delirium. Kate could see plainly what it was.

Nora's personal diary. No more. No less.

A single-page entry wrought by the hand of a woman who made a decision, a decision that would change everything. And there it was, in all its glory, to push Kate over the edge of grief and confusion. To surprise her.

To ruin everything.

Chapter 19—Amelia

Clara had left for work. Kate was nowhere to be found. It felt like they were back to the drawing board with plans.

That would be all well and good if Amelia didn't need to get back to New York. She had tips to earn and, maybe, a part to prepare for. The whole estate thing was turning into a bigger project than she'd have liked.

And now, with Clara acting despondent... the immediate future did not look bright.

Megan agreed, complaining in no uncertain terms that morning over coffee.

"Do you think she wants the cottage?" Megan asked, narrowing her eyes on Amelia suspiciously.

Amelia took a sip, and it scalded her tongue. She winced. "I have no idea. I think she just wants... normalcy. Right? I mean, don't we all?"

Megan rolled her eyes. "I don't see normalcy in our immediate future. We've only just begun uncovering issues with all this."

Amelia considered her sister's suggestion. "What do you mean 'all this'?"

"Mom's estate. Clara and Kate teaming up. Our past. All of it. We don't even know what else is going to turn up from here on out. That lawyer acted like his four leather binders would answer everything. No. Too pat. Too neat. Especially for Nora."

A defensive prickle climbed up Amelia's spine, though she wasn't sure who to defend. Poor handsome Michael? The man with his life together who was just trying to do his job? Or their mom, for weaving a web of secrets and promptly dying before a final showdown. "Michael's just trying to help," she started, trying again on her coffee, this time with more success. "And Mom was from a different time. A different era. She didn't live her life online for the whole world to see. Of course we have to claw through some cobwebs." Amelia involuntarily rested her gaze on Megan's phone.

Tucking it away into her sweater pocket, Megan answered smoothly, "I beg to differ."

"Oh?" Amelia replied, slurping down half her mug. She was going to need at least three more pots to make it through that day. Jimmy's insistent presence. A problem with the estate. And now Megan, dredging up old wounds.

"When a woman puts her kids to work on her income projects while she flounces about at a country club for the weekend, I think it's safe to say she is living out loud. Or... *was*, as the case may be."

Shaking her head, Amelia couldn't help but grin. "Touché."

Kate and Megan carried hard feelings over how much they had to work growing up. Amelia, however, had enjoyed it. Perhaps, she was afraid to admit she was a little more like their mother. A little more interested in a publicly glamorous life, the same kind that Nora made happen. Did she pull it off by slave-driving her daughters?

Yes.

Did Amelia mind?

No.

Work hard, play hard. It was the adage Amelia had looked forward to most about growing up. Whenever that time came.

***

"I got a text from Kate." Megan reappeared from the bathroom, her face scrubbed clean of the usual black eyeliner and pallid setting powder. She looked, for once, *alive*. Vulnerable, even.

Amelia smiled at her. "What did she say?"

"She had to run an errand. Something to do with Matt." The two grinned at each other. "She said for us to go to Michael's office and get the ball rolling with the appeal."

"Can we do that without her?" Amelia asked, unhooking the leash from Dobi's collar and letting him race free throughout the small living room. She'd never seen him as energetic as he'd been in Birch Harbor. Lakeside living suited him. Even in a little bungalow.

"I don't know, but I'm not sitting around here waiting. If we aren't moving on this, then I'm going back home. Sarah has been texting me nonstop. Brian can't cook to save his life, and she's stuck there alone with him."

"I could think of worse people to be stuck alone with," Amelia replied, grabbing her purse off the counter.

Megan frowned. "Oh, yeah? Like Jimmy?"

A cackle erupted out of Amelia's mouth, and she quickly quelled it, bewildered by the outburst. "Sorry. I—I have no idea where that came from."

"I made a joke. A sort of mean joke. You laughed. That's where it came from."

Amelia shook her head and started toward the door. "Yeah, thanks. I get it. I just meant—"

"Oh, no. I know what you meant. You meant that you didn't want to laugh at Jimmy and your joke of a relationship."

Amelia whipped around, ready to start a fight, but Megan held her hands up in apology. "Sorry. I'm sorry. That was harsh. True, but harsh."

"No, I understand, actually. All of you hate Jimmy. Even Dobi hates Jimmy. I'm embarrassed now that I left the poor guy with him. But... "

"Oh, here we go. More excuses. Amelia, girl. Own it. If you're going to stay with him, then stop apologizing for him. Stop giving credit to *our* feelings and start giving credit to *yours*. Yes, we don't like him. We think you should end it. But if you won't end it, then at least stand up for him. Fight for him. Make us *like* him."

Taken aback that Megan was, in some bizarre way, validating Jimmy (or, at least, Amelia's stick-to-itiveness with Jimmy), Amelia cracked a grin. "I think I know where this is coming from," she answered as they left Clara's house and headed to Megan's SUV.

"Oh yeah? Where?"

"Your dirty little secret," Amelia replied, pinning Megan with a meaningful look.

Megan shook her head. "I don't have any dirty secrets. I'm honest as they come."

"Okay, then spill. What are you doing with the dating app?"

Megan shook her black hair back off her shoulders and pointed her key fob at the vehicle. But Amelia wasn't going to take a beep for an answer. She didn't get in on the passenger side. Instead, she stood in front of the SUV with her arms crossed.

Hesitating at the driver's side door, Megan cocked her head. "Nothing. That's what."

With that, the raven-haired Hannigan hopped in the front seat and revved the engine.

Amelia wasn't intimidated by this menacing show of force. Yet, she believed Megan. Her sisters might be imperfect and oddball. But they were honest.

Which, by all accounts, set them apart from their mother.

The late, great Nora Hannigan. Queen of the Country Club. Mother of Girls. Manipulator Extraordinaire.

That was Nora. But that was not her daughters.

***

They pulled up outside the family law offices, and Megan threw the SUV into park.

"I really don't think we're going to make any headway without Kate. She's the executor," Amelia protested as she chewed on a hangnail.

Megan shrugged. "We'll try. If we get nowhere, then I'll send Kate an emergency text."

With that, they headed in together, Megan in front, pumping her arms purposefully into the quaint building as Amelia strode behind.

"Oh, it's the Hannigan sisters," the secretary cooed from her perch down below a tall reception desk.

Megan answered first. "Stevenson. Megan Stevenson."

Sharon made a face at Megan's correction. "Sorry about that. I didn't mean to overstep."

"She'll be back to Hannigan soon, anyway," Amelia added helpfully, but Megan threw her a look. "What?" Amelia asked her sister before stage-whispering to the secretary, "She's getting a divorce."

"Now that's a darn shame." The woman stood behind the desk and wrung her hands in front of her ample bosom. "I'm terribly sorry to hear it. Divorce is worse than death, they say. I wouldn't know. My Harry and I have been together since the war."

Amelia stifled a giggle. Whatever war that woman could possibly be talking about made no sense. And even if it did, using war as a context for the birth of a marriage felt morbid, at best.

She cut in, trying to divert the conversation appropriately. "Ma'am, we're hoping to see Mr. Matuszewski."

Michael Matuszewski wasn't originally from Birch Harbor. His family, however, was. Amelia wondered why he'd come to Birch Harbor at all. Was Detroit overrun with lawyers? Did this guy spend every weekend at the lake? Amelia wondered quite a lot about him.

"Ladies, hello." His familiar, warm voice boomed at the edge of the hallway. Amelia and Megan looked up.

"Hi," Megan said, waving a rigid hand.

Amelia smiled. "Hi, Michael." She could have sworn his eyes lingered on her a moment longer than was appropriate, for their particular circumstances or any, really. Between veritable strangers, a lingering look was almost always indecent. What mattered was whether it was welcome.

Amelia decided it was.

"I was expecting Kate this morning. Are you here waiting for her?"

Megan glanced back at Amelia, and they turned to him together, Megan taking the lead. "Yes and no. Kate sent us ahead of her to reopen the conversation."

"Come on back. I expected as much." He waved them toward his office, more casually than the day before. Now, despite the early hour, Michael wore his sleeves rolled up to his elbows. His hair was a little less gelled and a little messier. Still, however, he radiated power and control. Two things Amelia had never known a man to possess. After all, she was reared by a strong woman. Their dad had left the picture before Amelia even got to high school.

"Clara," he began, once they were seated orderly around his desk.

Amelia frowned and glanced at Megan. "Pardon?" she asked.

"You're going to contest on Clara's behalf, I presume?"

"Yes," Megan answered this time, her posture rigid and voice assured. "We'd like to discuss rearranging some things based on the fact that she was entirely left out. And, well, she *was* Nora's daughter, I mean."

Michael arched an eyebrow but answered evenly. "Sure. I understand. With Kate's blessing, we can move to arrange the proper paperwork in contest against the terms of the estate. Is she on her way, or...?"

Megan and Amelia looked at each other. "She will be, yes," Amelia replied as Megan pulled her phone from her pocket and tapped away on a text message.

"Should we come back?" Amelia asked, her eyes on Michael now, studying his features, his sharp, lawyerly jaw. His deep gray eyes. He *looked* like a lawyer. But not, maybe, a small-town lawyer.

"No, no. I am free this morning. Other than an afternoon meeting with the town council, I'm all yours." There it was. Amelia was positive. He was examining her just as she was examining him. She suddenly felt aware of her crow's feet. Her bare face and flat hair. Digging in her purse for her lip gloss would be an obvious maneuver. One only an insecure woman would enact.

Her heart thudded in her chest as Megan fumbled with the phone just inches away, but Amelia reached into the deepest recesses of everything she knew about acting and pulled out the confidence of a starlet. A top-billed actress. A Lady Macbeth, even.

"Michael, tell me. What brought you to Birch Harbor originally?" She pricked up the corner of her lip and dipped her chin only just, glaring through her naked, dark eyelashes.

He faltered a bit, and Amelia felt good. Better than she'd ever felt with Jimmy. "My family," he answered, anchoring his jaw in his hand on top of his desk. She had his full attention.

Amelia's eyes fell on the lower half of his face. The stubble and full lips. White teeth. "Your parents... or?"

"Yes. This practice was my grandfather's, actually. My dad moved away and never looked back. But, well, I was curious, and I love the history of the place."

He was about to carry on, and Amelia was entirely enraptured, but Megan broke in.

"Amelia," she said, her voice ice cold. "Kate wrote back. She can't come. She, um—" Megan flicked her eyes up at Michael before staring hard at her sister. "We need to go. Now."

Chapter 20—Nora

April 4, 1992

The doctor just left.

The girls are fine. That's as much as I'll say there.

As for Wendell, well... Wendell is... accepting. He's accepting, though I don't know why. I feel angry. Everything was perfect before. Now this. I could punch a hole in the wall, I could. Where was I?

It's like a recurring dream, but the faces are different.

It's my fault. I had control and lost it. I let it slip through my fingertips. I was distracted, admittedly. All the work. And all the play. Wendell is mad at me, probably. He should be. I deserve it. IT. Now it's become a monster. I can't allow that. It is not an it. Oh! He? She?

Wendell says leave "it" alone. Let go and let God! He's fine with embracing the natural course of events. He loves me. He loves the girls. To him, there's nothing more. No reason for a big, bad change. But he has not been down this road before. Not like me.

Lord, Your will is what got us here. I hate to even write this, but I can't bear it, Lord. You've slapped me in the face. It's unacceptable. Unsustainable. Unfair. Un-everything, Lord.

And yet, I trust You.

Besides! I'm Nora Hannigan, and You made me a planner, and so I have a plan.

Arizona, where Roberta lives. She's my sister. She'll help. I haven't spoken with her yet, because Wendell won't go. I'm not sure he'll want us to go, either. He says if I go and take the girls then he'll stay with his parents. It feels like a threat, but it's not.

He refuses to be alone, of course. He hates to be alone. Maybe that's why he doesn't mind this little surprise, this little intrusion. The more the merrier. It's something Wendell says.

I would say it, too, if I hadn't already been down this dark and deathly road. I would say it if it were true! But these things never turn out merrily. You know it as well as I do. That's why it's a commandment, right, Lord? That's why you punished me before.

But I can't stay. Not now. I might come back. If things fall into place, I might come back and resume this life, if Wendell won't mind if I change the story. I have to change the story.

But if I don't change the story, what will I do? Or what if Roberta won't have us? Should we even be traveling? That's a question for the doctor.

Maybe I'll buy another place. Something away from town, inland. A farm or something. Or, I could go to Arizona, after all. I could do both! My God, we have the money now. I could do both! Wendell won't mind a new project. He loves it. He loves us. He wants us to be happy. No, he probably doesn't care about the shame, but I care. I care for us.

Chapter 21—Megan

Sweeping Amelia out of the office and into the sunny Michigan morning, Megan spoke in hushed tones.

"Kate opened the letter. And *that's* why she's with Matt."

Amelia's eyes grew wide. "What was in the letter? How do you know?"

"Well, I don't know for *sure*. But why else would she skip the meeting? I think it's obviously about Clara. And, that's where we are going. Kate said to meet her at Matt's house."

Shaking her head, Amelia spit a few curses. "Why couldn't Mom just add Clara to the will? What was the problem with that?"

"I don't know," Megan replied. "Hopefully we're about to find out."

***

Heading to Matt's house was no easy task. He lived on Heirloom Island, a tiny chunk of land that floated southeast of town, adjacent to Heirloom Cove. They'd first have to go to the ferry, then sit there and grow nauseous for the next half an hour until spilling onto shore amid smells of the ferryman's sweat-slicked sunscreen and the flapping fumes of a variety of lake birds. The Birch Harbor Ferry wasn't known for its glamour. It could probably use a makeover, Megan thought to herself.

But as she sat there, next to Amelia, chewing on her thumbnail and imagining the sort of news that Kate was unwilling to reveal on the phone or via text—the sort of news that demanded they take a damn *ferry*, Megan thought of something else.

There were a *ton* of people in town. For May, the number seemed significant. Tourists by the droves. Cute bikini-clad girls and handsome tanned guys vying for attention from each other. Some in groups laughing, some paired off, canoodling in the far corners of the boat. It was fascinating. Megan felt like she was a fly on the wall of *The Bachelor* on location at Lake Huron, Michigan.

Once the ferry docked, Megan and Amelia hung back, waiting for the crowd to thin before them.

Amelia gripped Megan's hand. "Should we have called Clara?"

"No," Megan answered, firm. "Let's wait to see what Kate says. Maybe something *good* happened." Megan wasn't usually the optimistic type, but who knew? Kate and Matt out on the island instead of holed up in that mahogany and leather office? Maybe something good *had* happened.

They strode along the deck and up to the parking lot, where Kate said she'd meet them. Sure enough, the figure of a slender woman stood erect at the crest of the slight hill, her hand casting a shadow over her face so as to ease the reflection of the sun from off the water.

Kate waved, her fingers flashing up in a lackluster cascade. "Hey," she said once they were close. "Matt's house is just up the shore." She pointed back toward a pretty Victorian.

"Wow," Megan replied. "I didn't know he lived on the island."

"Moved here a few years back. After his divorce."

Megan and Amelia raised their eyebrows to one another before following Kate on foot less than a mile to his home. Kate didn't turn around, preferring instead to walk quietly in front of them.

Once there, Megan noticed Matt, pacing his front porch, one hand pushed through his hair, the other gripping a cell phone against his head.

"Is everything okay?" Megan asked, a feeling of alarm clenching her gut.

Kate stopped at the front lawn and waited for them to catch up before answering. "Yes and no. Everyone is fine. But there's been... a revelation."

"And Matt is in on this?" Amelia asked, hooking a finger toward him.

Nodding solemnly, Kate let out a sigh. "Yep. Now you two will be. I had to come to him first. I hope... I hope you'll understand."

Megan didn't, really. Her sisters were her blood. Not this local islander single dad who'd written off the Hannigans just as soon as they'd returned to Birch Harbor after their extended desert vacation.

At least, that was Megan's thirteen-year-old impression of things at the time.

The women strode to the porch, joining Matt as he thanked the person on the other end of the line before hanging up. "Hi, Megan. Amelia." He nodded his head to each in turn, and they said hello back.

"What's going on?" Amelia asked. Kate pressed her palms to her eyes and shook her head.

Matt stepped to her and set a hand on her shoulder awkwardly. Megan would have cringed at the gesture, if the situation didn't seem so dire.

"Let's go inside," he suggested, waving a hand back through a yawning front door.

They filed in and each found a spot at an industrial-style kitchen table—all wood and metal and screws beneath the rustic knotty top.

The next words out of Kate's mouth stunned Megan into silence.

"We can't contest the will."

Chapter 22—Kate

1992

The news had rocked the family. Their father had fallen quiet. Their mother turned to ice. Kate had no idea what her parents' private conversation consisted of.

All she knew is what happened next, a drawn-out succession of events. The last-minute road trip after a hushed phone call with their family doctor. The summer in Arizona with Aunt Roberta. A girls' summer, their mom had called it. That much proved true.

And of course, before all of that, the breakup with Matt: a tear-stained conversation where they went back and forth and back and forth, both pleading and pushing and blaming. Teen angst at its finest.

But none of that was the worst thing that happened that summer.

The worst thing was losing their dad. It made for a second secret. They returned home, the new baby having fussed and pooped and spat up the whole, long journey back, and he was gone.

At the time, Kate and her sisters believed their mother. They believed that he just... left, that the events of the summer pushed him over the edge.

But the thing of it was, Kate never read such a response in her father's reaction. She never saw hate or anger. Fear, maybe. But Nora had herded them so quickly out of there, that Kate had no clue what the poor man thought about it all.

Upon their return, there were meetings—important ones. She remembered that part as well as anything else. Nora had visited the Actons. The Actons had been in touch with authorities. Everyone settled on a loose agreement: that Wendell Acton took off. Nora eventually painted him a deadbeat, but Kate never felt the woman had believed that. It didn't make sense, for one, that Nora Hannigan would marry a deadbeat, and, for two, that Nora Hannigan believed her husband had, all of a sudden, turned into a deadbeat. Whatever happened to Wendell Acton rested deep in the heart of Birch Harbor lore. And there it would stay.

Kate never did decide if her father's fate was related to their vacation. She didn't think her mother capable of—or interested in—anything insidious. But the timing was too odd. Or, too perfect. He wasn't *that* mad. Not to Kate or anyone else.

After the whole thing, the Actons dismissed Nora and her daughters entirely. Holing up in their house, the old, antiquated Birch Harbor lighthouse on the lake, like recluses, until their dying days years later. Kate suspected that her grandparents held her mom accountable. Even Kate sort of held her mom accountable. Amelia and Megan cast blame, too.

But, with time, the town forgot about it. Accepting that some men just leave. And, Wendell Acton was one such man.

Yet, there was a hole in the theory, a detail the investigators and the family didn't piece together then and maybe never would.

It wasn't just Wendell who went missing, it was some of his belongings, too.

Things the Hannigans wouldn't know were missing until years later, when Kate was rummaging around in the basement of the house on the harbor, laying claim to the treasures left to her by their late mother's estate. An estate so finely tuned, that no one had questioned its flaws. Its inaccuracies.

Kate never would find her father's wristwatch.

Chapter 23—Amelia

"Are you going to show us?" Amelia asked, her voice so quiet she didn't think Kate had heard her.

Matt pushed the envelope across the table, his eyes on Kate, who nodded.

Megan leaned in, and Amelia carefully slid out a thin, narrow page from the envelope.

"Is this her...?"

"Her diary, yes," Kate answered. "At least, I think so."

Together, Amelia and Megan read the slanted, even script—their mother's careful handwriting, handwriting she'd taken seriously in her years of grammar school. Handwriting she had flaunted during Country Club fundraisers when they asked *who will make the sign?* and at town council meetings when they asked *will anyone put together thank-you notes?*

Amelia's eyes moved across the words, but none of them made sense. If what she was reading was true, then they had lived a lie, and for what? If what that journal said was true, then the will *was* valid. Precluding the date of the Heirloom house, of course.

Her pulse quickened and her breath caught in her throat as she finished and looked up at Kate, first. Then, Matt. Finally, Megan.

It was Megan who spoke next. "Is this *real*?"

Kate shrugged then dropped her head to her chest.

Matt answered. "As far as we know, yes. We called the county recorder's office here and in Arizona. I just got off the phone when you two showed up. I talked to the record keeper at Birch Harbor Unified, too."

"And what do they say?" Amelia asked, floored, still.

Kate lifted her head. Lines crossed each other above her head. The hollows beneath her eyes sat deep and sallow. "They didn't know about anything. Mom lied to me. To us."

"That's what they said?" Amelia asked, bewildered.

"No, that isn't what they said." Matt reached his hand out and covered Kate's. Amelia shifted in her seat, unable to tear her eyes away from the equally familiar and foreign display of modest affection.

"So what did they say? Get to the point." Megan's neck glowed red and splotchy. Amelia shook her head sorrowfully.

"They said," Kate began to answer, searching Matt's face. "They said the truth. Somehow, we just never found out."

Chapter 24—Clara

Teaching all day was exactly what Clara needed. It would distract her from the business of contesting the will.

It would also give her a chance to be away from her sisters and really think about their question. *What did she want*?

First period was a blur, a mess of papers and excuses for not having papers and following up on the sub's notes. By the time second period began, Clara finally had a chance to sit at her desk, check emails, and sip coffee.

Her students sat quietly, completing their bell work, and Clara knocked out a flurry of housekeeping messages; there would be an assembly on Friday; tardy lunch students were being rerouted to the library; ticket prices for the promotion dance were going up, up, up! *Get yours today!*

It reminded Clara of her own middle school experience. The hope of being asked to a dance. The nervousness about starting high school.

Most kids who had older siblings, enjoyed something of a paved road—for better or worse. Amelia had it harder. Teachers had loved Kate. Or at least, that was Clara's impression. To follow in her footsteps was to succeed a lovable queen to the throne. But then Amelia, with her creative energy and free spirit, set the bar low for Megan. Megan, more Type A but less lovable, simply enjoyed the experience of knowing almost everyone who was in the upper grades. It offered her a buffer. A reputation.

Then came Clara, twelve years younger than Megan. Most of her sisters' teachers were retired or long gone by then, and no students had ever heard of a Hannigan child. They only knew about the Hannigan family. The earliest settlers of the area. The name was more like a story than an identifier of real people. It had turned Clara into an only child with a history. An odd thing to be.

Now, as she sat at her computer, finished with emails, neat stacks of papers to grade towering to the left of her keyboard, she felt an itch.

A list-making itch. Not the pros/cons type. More like the goal-setting type of list she'd forced her churlish students to compose months back at the start of the second semester.

She pushed her keyboard aside and pulled open the small notebook she kept for her personal notes. Shuffling through a few pages of shopping lists and one to-do list, she landed on a blank page with thin pink lines running orderly across.

At the top, Clara titled it: *Personal Goals*.

Beneath that, she pushed the tip of her Ticonderoga onto the start of a new line—a new word... a new sentence... *anything*.

But nothing came.

She flipped the page. On the next blank sheet, she added a different title: *Hannigan Estate.*

Beneath that, she found her rhythm, jotting down each of the four properties and even some of the belongings she recalled from the reading of the will. Lastly, she added a few mementos she had wanted to keep for herself, such as her grandmother's afghans and a hope chest that she once heard about but never did see with her own two eyes.

Beside each item, she listed who she felt best matched with each property. To Clara, it didn't make sense to sell the house on the harbor. At least, not yet. It was too important. Too historic. But also, too much work. Perhaps Kate was a good fit? She needed to move anyway. Of course, she'd wanted to downsize, but that was just because of the mortgage payment. If she had the house, then Ben and Will could visit. Megan's daughter, Sarah, too.

Clara didn't know what made sense for Megan. She was on the verge of divorce. Maybe she'd be better off with the house? Amelia was least likely to handle it. But she could handle *something*. She could handle low-maintenance rentals... like The Bungalows.

Would anyone want the cottage?

Clara thought back to what she knew of the cottage's modest beginnings. Apparently, it was something that her mother and father began working on in the months leading up to Clara's birth.

From what Kate had told her, Clara knew that Nora had asked Wendell to find, purchase, and break ground on a new home inland, something lower maintenance. And, he did. Of course, his project went unfinished, but Nora forged ahead, hiring people here and there and chipping in herself to pull off completion of the modest, pretty three-bedroom, two-bath that sat next to Birch Creek.

Then, nothing. With Wendell's absence, the cottage sat there, collecting dust and overflowing clothes and furniture for a long time, until Nora decided to move in herself, leaving the place on the lake for one with easier daily upkeep, apparently.

It was a short walk to the school. So short, indeed, that sometimes Clara would steal away inside the cottage by herself and snuggle into the single iron frame bed that made its way there. In that bed, Clara would read and drift in and out of sleep until nighttime drew near, at which point she'd hurry home to an almost empty house.

Clara snapped to attention, inhaling sharply.

Yes. The cottage.

That's what Clara needed.

The cottage with the afghans and the iron bed. The cottage that had been her hideaway for so long.

The cottage that was denied to her when Nora wanted her to live at The Bungalows and play property manager.

She needed the cottage.

It was settled.

After a quick set of directions to her students to put away their grammar textbooks and take out their journals, Clara tapped out a text message to the group chat with her sisters. She knew she'd be interrupting their meeting with Michael, but they had to have the information. They had to know to give her the cottage. Nothing else. Just the cottage.

All Clara needed was the cottage. If she could get that, then she wouldn't necessarily have what she *wanted*, but she could figure it out. Clara Hannigan could solve the world's problems in that little place on the creek. She did as a kid. She would do it as an adult.

Clara would move to the cottage on the creek, and that is where she would figure out her life—away from the big house, away from the four-plex, away from the loud lake and the tourists and the noise of town. In her own little cottage.

Where maybe she could find that hope chest.

Chapter 25—Kate

Kate had always thought her life was defined squarely by two phases: before she had children and after. This is what everyone had led her to believe, and it's what she indeed knew to be true.

After all, giving birth and taking on the role of motherhood was life changing.

Once Ben and Will were born and Kate and Paul had found their new normal—their lasting normal, by all accounts—phase two finally began in earnest. Kate took solace in raising her little family, and found the chance to part with Nora, Amelia, Megan, and even sweet little Clara to be easier than she'd ever imagined.

Living all the way up on Apple Tree Hill, away from Birch Harbor, didn't hurt, either. There, she'd made a new life. She paid bills, changed diapers, and organized mother meetings in her front room. There, she washed the dishes every night and sorted and stowed fresh laundry each morning. Then, once the boys left for college, life tipped again. She was still, of course, their mom. And at that point, she was also still a wife.

New normal became book club and floral arrangements and gardening. Then, eventually, Kate discovered the working world. First with a secretarial position at the sanitation company Paul managed. Then as an underling at an upstart realty company. Currently, she was still very much an underling, since during Paul's sickness and subsequent death she was forced to take so much time off that she had to start over again from the beginning when she'd finally grieved enough to return.

Kate had always predicted she'd one day become a comfortable widow far down the road and well into old age. Comfortable financially, thanks to wise investments and helpful children. Comfortable in her new town, which always somehow felt like a new town. Never a hometown.

But she was stripped of that luxury. No comfort. Too young. Too mired in debt from *poor* investments and expensive college tuition times two. Of course, Ben and Will were worth every penny. But she'd like to have some money to spare. Some to cover the mortgage on the house the boys had grown up in, for starters.

Then again, even that felt wrong. Kate didn't actually want to stay in that beautiful house with casement windows and high ceilings and a lush garden. She wanted soul.

She wanted a home. And, in fact, Birch Harbor was the only home she'd ever known, even if it came with the heartache that a true home often knew.

The two phases of her life—before children and after—weren't the full story. It would appear that there was about to be a third phase: The Great Unknown. The preview to her golden years, should she be lucky enough to enjoy them. And, the handling of her mother's death and her needful sisters. But God didn't stop there, no sir. He had to throw in a monkey wrench. A twist. A problem.

Kate's biggest worry for the moment was not, in fact, sharing the truth with Clara.

It was whether Amelia and Megan were going to cooperate in light of that truth.

Then again, perhaps the letter, that sweet, sickening letter, meant they wouldn't have to. Maybe, just maybe, there was another way out.

Presently, she and her sisters sat at Matt's table, their lips in tight lines and eyebrows furrowed heavily.

Kate spoke. "I'll take the cottage. We'll split the house, since it wasn't mentioned. You two can fight over The Bungalows and the land. That's the plan, okay?" She started to pull her hand away from Matt, but something stopped her. "Speaking of which," she continued, slipping her hand out from his and returning it primly to her lap. "What did you plan to offer for the house, Matt?"

She felt Amelia's and Megan's eyes bore a hole in her, and she caught Matt's uncomfortable reaction. But this was down to brass tacks. The will—and Clara's exclusion from it—was irrelevant if they could fetch a pretty penny on the sale of the house. Or, at least, find another option that would provide Clara with *something*.

He cleared his throat. "Kate," he started, holding up his hands defensively. "I'm not sure now is the time to discuss that. Are you sure you want to sell it?"

"You showed up there, right?" Megan pressed, suddenly on Kate's side.

He nodded. "Yes, but, I didn't... I didn't realize things were sticky. I would never want to intrude. If I can help, then I will help. But I'm not about to come between you three—or, um... you *four*. And that place is a legend. I mean... " He was rambling, and it made Kate smile. He always used to ramble, even as a teenager, a fumbling teenager who asked permission to so much as kiss Kate on the cheek.

"Listen, I'd be happy if we sell it. I'm in New York now, and—" Amelia was on the precipice of launching into some well-meaning lecture about her unavailability and big dreams and high hopes, but Megan cut her off.

"Oh, please. Amelia, you haven't had a real part since you left Lincoln, Nebraska. Nothing is keeping you in New York, and you know it."

Kate's eyes widened in horror as her sisters opened the same argument that they'd gone rounds with since the funeral.

Amelia put up a good fight. "I have Jimmy. And Dobi. And a great studio apartment," she protested.

Megan rolled her eyes, landing them squarely on Kate. "Are you hearing what I'm hearing? She actually plans to stay in the city?"

Kate shook her head. "I never thought she was *leaving* the city. And why do *you* care, Ms. Suburbia?"

Megan clicked her tongue. "I'm not sticking around there. Not unless I get the house, and even then... well, I'll probably sell it."

"So you're coming back to Birch Harbor?" Kate pressed.

"Maybe," Megan replied. "Maybe I'll take the cottage. It's the right size for Sarah and me, and then... just me, once Sarah graduates."

"You're not taking the cottage," Kate answered, her eyes narrowing on Megan, her spine lengthening into a rod.

Matt held his palms up at the three of them. "Ladies, come on. We have bigger fish to fry than who gets what, right?" His eyebrows twisted up and he looked at Kate. She swallowed and her body relaxed.

But he was wrong. Nora's letter, the revelation, the truth, and the will—all it came down to was *who* was getting *what*.

And Matt was now part of the puzzle, but he didn't seem to realize it.

Chapter 26—Nora

June 9, 1992

Wendell phoned yesterday. Or should I say I phoned him. He found a little house on Birch Creek. It's a fix-it-upper, he says. He also says it's full of charm and that it reminds him of me. It's incomplete, though. It has a back building, a barn I think. Lots more construction to become whole, I guess.

I'm not sure that he'll make an offer, but I hope so. I'm in no state to make big decisions. That much is true.

If we get the house on the creek, then I'll feel better. I'll feel like we have options when we return. The girls can stay at the cottage while things blow over. Maybe all the moving and shaking will distract everyone and paint us as eccentrics. I always wanted to be an eccentric, until I married Wendell. I could have been Miss Havisham herself if it weren't for my loving husband and wayward children.

I told Wendell what I thought was best regarding our family's little situation. He didn't seem to understand. He didn't see "what the big deal" was. Wendell's heart knows no shame. I envy him for that.

All I have ever known are the scales of shame. My life has always been weighed on them.

I am going to live through this, and I will do it right. I won't be ashamed, not of the situation. In fact, no matter how hard it is, this will all be a blessing. A blessing. I'm sure of it.

Chapter 27—Clara

The lunch bell rang at the same time Clara's phone buzzed against the metal pencil tray in her desk drawer.

She'd forced herself to keep her focus on her classes. She'd forced herself to ignore the background drama of the estate.

Now, it seemed, she'd get some news.

Mercy Hennings was dawdling at her desk, and Clara hated to shoo the nervous little thing out, but she had to answer the call.

"Mercy," she began, her phone crooked at the ready in her hand, "are you staying in here for lunch… or?"

"Oh, no, Miss Hannigan. I just wanted to let you know that my dad said thanks for meeting him in the parking lot yesterday. And, well, I suppose I wanted to say thanks, too."

"It was no problem. We just happened to bump into each other is all," Clara replied warmly as the incoming phone call went to voicemail. "Well, have a nice lunch, Mercy."

"Thanks. You too." The child smiled sadly, and Clara's teacher instinct kicked into overdrive.

"Mercy, is everything okay?"

The girl turned on her heel and bit her lower lip. "Oh, yeah. Kind of." She kept her eyes on the hardwood planks of the classroom floor.

"Oh, sweetheart, come here. Sit down. What's bothering you?" Clara waved a hand to the student chair next to her desk, and Mercy eased down into it, her backpack sliding off her shoulder.

Clara eyed the backpack, then her phone and asked Mercy for a moment to send a text. She quickly wrote to Kate explaining she'd be in touch in five minutes. Just five minutes to solve the problems of the world for a middle-schooler. Guilt tugged at Clara's heart.

"It's just that high school is coming up, and I'm scared."

Relaxing into her own seat, Clara smiled. "What are you scared about, Mercy?"

"The other kids, mostly." Mercy fell into a hunch and crossed her arms over her chest.

Clara replied with some confusion. "What do you mean? You know almost everyone who will be in your freshman class."

Mercy sighed a deep, adolescent sigh, her upper lip catching briefly on her braces.

Clara suppressed a grin.

"I mean the private school kids from the island."

Nodding knowingly, Clara answered with a wise, "Ahh. Yes." On Heirloom Island, just southeast of the house Clara had grown up in, stretched a small water-locked chunk of earth, complete with its own private school. An island with a private school made for special circumstances. Of those children who lived on the island, there were two types who opted out of St. Mary's: too poor to stay and pay for the Catholic school or too heathen to have any interest in applying for a scholarship. And as for those children who lived on the mainland, there were also two types of children: normal and just heathen enough to beg off the ferry ride to school or Catholic and rich enough to afford and even enjoy the exclusive day trip to get an education on an *island*.

But that trouble only lasted through eighth grade. So far, the Catholic school on the island didn't offer grades nine through twelve. This meant that all those little private school teens would flood Birch Harbor High.

"I get it," Clara went on. And she did. "Tell you what, Mercy. If you get to ninth grade and start having friend trouble, you come tell me. I'll help, okay?"

Mercy nodded gratefully and collected her backpack. *Problem solved.*

"Okay, Miss Hannigan. Thank you."

The girl hesitated at the door, just as Clara was about to hit CALL on Kate's contact details. "Yes, Mercy?"

Mercy ran her tongue over her lower lip, freeing it from another catch on her braces. "My dad said you're really pretty."

***

Amelia answered Kate's phone. "Hey," she said, her voice betraying some sense that things were not going according to plan.

"Hey," Clara echoed. "How's it going?"

"Well, we aren't at Michael's office."

"Oh?" Clara asked, a pit growing in the bottom of her stomach and washing away a smile from the compliment she'd just received.

Amelia cleared her throat and waited a beat before answering. "Everything is totally fine, though. Something came up, but it's actually okay. Seriously."

Clara felt flushed, and she stood to pace the rows of student desks as she pressed Amelia for details. "What did the lawyer say? Do we have grounds to contest still? We do, right?"

"Like I said, Clara. Something came up. The appeal... ah... well, we are shifting direction."

"Can I talk to Kate?" Clara asked, her voice pinched as she held her breath, waiting for her oldest sister, her most grown-up one.

"Hi, Clara," Kate's voice came on the phone, smooth and reassuring. "Listen, we can't contest the will anymore. But we're all here talking and we realize that we do need to get some clarification on what we can do with mom's property. Everything is going to be fine. I don't want you to worry, but let's plan to meet at the house on the harbor after you're done with school. I'll have Matt order a pizza, okay?"

Clara frowned. "Matt? Matt who?"

"Oh, right," Kate answered, murmuring something away from the line before coming back on. "Matt Fiorillo. Um, he's here, too."

Before Clara could ask why, Kate had passed the phone off to Megan like they were playing a long-distance game of hot potato.

"Can *you* tell me what's going on?" Clara asked Megan, her tone revealing her anxiety and impatience. She felt so left out and in the dark. It was like their childhood all over again. Clara so much younger, so much different, so much apart from her older sisters. Part of her wished Mercy had stayed behind to have lunch in the classroom. Then, at least, Clara wouldn't feel so lonely.

"All I can say," Megan answered, "is that Kate is fighting for you."

Clara figured Megan meant it as a kindness, that Kate was "fighting" for her. But then, did it also imply that Amelia and Megan... were not?

Chapter 28—Amelia

"We have a couple of hours. What do we need to do to get everything in order?" Amelia asked earnestly after Matt cleared away their glasses of iced tea. Tensions had cooled, but there was a lot left to do and discuss. And, even minor issues awaited them back on the mainland. For Amelia, those included Dobi's potty break and Jimmy's looming existence. He'd texted her throughout the morning, commenting on where he was and what he was up to. Somehow, he'd made his way to the house on the harbor, though he promised her he'd stick to Birch Village until she was back at the house.

Megan, too, was fighting against urgency. Sarah needed her to return home that night. Although, Amelia wondered if that was true or if Megan *wanted* to return home. Or, at least, return to her daughter and husband.

Kate seemed distracted more than ever. Amelia felt for her. Here Kate was, in control of their mom's affairs on the heels of her own personal tragedy—losing Paul not too long before. Plus, Amelia knew Kate's financial situation was not much better than her own. Or Megan's for that matter. The only one who enjoyed any degree of stability at the present was Clara, of all people.

The financial pressure along with an extended run-in with Kate's high school sweetheart only added to their drama. Being sequestered in Birch Harbor until they hammered out the details felt like bunking up in a crucible. Something—or someone—was about to burst.

A thought occurred to Amelia, an off-topic detail, altogether, but one that perhaps mattered. "Do you live here alone?" she asked Matt, staring around the walls. "Or do you have a roommate?" She fixed her gaze on Megan, who caught on to her line of reasoning.

"I live here with my daughter," he answered.

Kate cocked her head at Amelia as if to say *see? No scandal.*

Amelia smiled. "How old is your daughter? What's her name?"

"She's fourteen. Viviana." He plucked a photo from his fridge and showed it to them. Each sister cooed in turn.

"She's beautiful. Does she live with you full-time?" Kate asked.

Matt nodded. "Yep. Her mom moved to Detroit chasing some big-city gig. She's very successful. She visits often."

"If you died today," Amelia went on, narrowing down to her main point and question—they had figured he had a daughter, that was no big mystery, "who would get this place?"

"Viviana," he answered easily. "Why?"

"Well," Amelia replied, her emerging claim surfacing on her lips like she was morphing into some sort of intellectual detective, "what about your ex? And your parents? Would they get in the way at all?"

He laughed derisively. "No, of course not. Everything would go to Viviana... or—" his voice fell away, and he looked at Kate.

Chapter 29—Kate

Her face softened at Matt. Kate didn't know Viviana. She'd only ever seen the girl at the funeral, and, while she knew Matt had moved on from their adolescent romance, his new life was a hard pill to swallow. Then again, hadn't Kate moved on, too?

Yes.

Kate had moved on. She'd married and had two sons and lived a whole new life, worlds away.

So then, why did her pulse quicken when Matt covered her hand with his? Why did she go to him first, before her sisters?

There was no rule demanding that Kate seek out Matthew Fiorillo. Her mother hadn't left such a stipulation in her diary entry, after all.

But there they were, in his kitchen on Heirloom Island, like old friends. Perhaps that's exactly why she'd gone to him. Amelia and Megan were too removed from Birch Harbor. Matt, having stayed on there and experienced the waves of time in the small lakeside town, was a rock. More so than Kate's own sisters, apparently.

"Matt," she said, changing the conversation. "What have we missed?"

"What do you mean?" he asked.

Megan and Amelia had left the table and were currently wandering around in front of the house, giving Kate and Matt space to talk.

"I mean what has gone on in Birch Harbor all these years? What have you seen and heard?"

"What have I seen and heard about your mom and Clara?" he asked earnestly.

Kate blinked. "Well," she began, swallowing a growing lump in her throat. "Yeah."

He breathed in through his nose and pushed the air out of his mouth as he leaned back in his chair, a reflective glaze coating his stare. "Same old, same old, I suppose. I've seen your mom do her country club thing. I've seen her at the village. I've heard she's made her rounds at parties and big town events, sponsoring this or showing up for that." He lowered his voice for what he said next. "I've seen her with men."

Kate paled at his implication. Her heart hurt. Her body even hurt. She was supposed to be back home by now, packing her house and preparing to put it on the market. She was supposed to be sad and depressed that her mother was gone, not angry that her mother left something of a mess behind.

Inhaling sharply, she nodded in response. "And Clara? Do you ever see Clara?"

He shook his head sadly. "No. I think she keeps to herself."

Kate nodded again, this time more thoughtfully. "I'm sorry I dragged you into this, Matt. I'm sure you weren't expecting your high school girlfriend to rush in asking you to save her."

They locked eyes, and Matt leaned forward in his seat. He was the same boy she'd fallen in love with all those years ago, but now a man. His kind eyes sat inside of crow's feet and his chin and cheeks were shadowed by handsome stubble. And, Matt's mouth. A full mouth that had lived a lifetime away from hers. Back then, she'd have hated to think that Matt would belong to anyone but her.

But, he had. And not just romantically. His lips had no doubt kissed his own frail mother. His... daughter. Kate had missed all those moments with him. Were there more women, too? Was there someone... now?

"Matt," Kate whispered again. Just as she was about to apologize a second time, his jaw set and his eyes lowered to her lips.

"No," he whispered back. "I'm sorry. I'm sorry I didn't fight harder for you." A tear welled along her lower lash line. He lifted his thumb and reached across the table to brush it away. "Is it too late?"

***

She swallowed. It wasn't too late. But the timing was bad. She shook her head at Matt and blinked away the tears and thirty-some years' worth of regret. "We need to get ready to go. Clara will be done with school soon. I want to have a plan in place for this meeting." Kate stood abruptly from the table, and the air sucked out from between them, leaving in its wake a chill. "What do you have going on this afternoon? Do you have to pick up, um, Viviana from school, or...?"

"Or am I bringing pizza to the meeting of the minds?" he finished her sentence in a half-joke, and it successfully lightened the mood.

Kate grinned. "I did say that, didn't I?"

He nodded. "I can bring the pizza. Viviana walks home. She goes to St. Mary's just up the road. I'll leave a note for her. But, Kate—"

Folding her lips in between her teeth, she dipped her chin toward him. "Yes?"

"Are you sure I should come? This is a... this is awkward. It's a big conversation. Maybe a private one, even."

Kate glanced out the front window, her gaze falling on her younger sisters. She contemplated his point, mulling it over like she was smoothing a jagged rock in a tumbler.

Matt was right. The conversation was serious. It would be upsetting. It would be uncomfortable and confusing.

Two things needed to happen. And they needed to happen soon, so that the women could get back on with their lives. They needed to tell Clara the truth. And they needed to decide who was getting what.

And those conversations were inseparable, tied together in history and in the present, by all four of them. Matt belonged there, too. And if Clara were Amelia, who reveled in high drama and theatrics, then Kate would maybe bring him.

But Clara wasn't Amelia. She wasn't dramatic. She wasn't Megan either—tough and steel-willed. No. She was most like Kate, quiet, reserved, and generally serious. Mostly, Clara was still just a girl.

"Will you bring the pizza but wait outside? Perhaps in the back porch?" she asked Matt.

"Of course," he answered. "I'm good at that."

She cocked an eyebrow for clarification. "Good at what?"

He replied through a mischievous smile. "Waiting."

Chapter 30—Nora

October 4, 1992

With Wendell gone, I don't have the courage to be the woman I once was. My strength has left me. My neck seems to hurt every morning when I wake up. I'm sleeping on my stomach again, because I have no one to hold me at night.

There's only one way to honor Wendell, and it's done. Well, there was nothing technically "to do." And that's what Wendell wanted. For me to leave it alone.

So now here we are, with angry in-laws living up north, an unfinished cottage, an empty lot, the four-plex, a new baby, and this big old house that Wendell couldn't stomach to stay in alone.

I don't blame him.

There are secrets here, and they kissed our lives. He knew that, and I do. The girls probably sense it. But secrets can make things better.

Oh. Oh my. I just had an idea! I suppose writing in this old thing pays off after all.

Chapter 31—Megan

Amelia left the back yard and walked down to the shore to take a phone call—from Jimmy, no doubt.

Megan felt empty, lonely, too. She hadn't spoken to Sarah or Brian since she'd been in Birch Harbor, and she missed at least one of them.

Sarah didn't answer. She was still in class. Megan left a message asking her daughter to return her call. She needed to hear someone else's voice.

Before clicking off her phone, she rubbed her thumb up the screen, revealing Brian's name.

Without a second thought, Megan tapped it.

It rang. Anxiety crept up her arms, settling into her neck. Reluctantly, and yet, with a degree of giddiness, she pressed the device to her ear and waited.

Three rings later, his voice came on.

"Yeah," he said. Not a question. Not a greeting. Just a yeah.

"Um, hi. It's me." Megan waited a beat before adding, "Megan."

"I know," he replied. His tone matched the prickliness of his voice, and she immediately regretted calling.

Fumbling around for what to say next, she defaulted to what had become the most common topic of conversation. "I'm calling to check in on the settlement."

He sighed. "We're selling the house."

"What?" she asked, alarms filling her head. "What are you talking about? I thought either you or I would get it?"

"Lawyers think it's a dumb idea. We sell and split the profit, if there is any. Fresh slate. We can go our separate ways. You can follow your dream, for once."

"That's it?" She kicked herself for the way she'd asked it. She sounded weak and desperate. Like she *wanted* the fight to go on.

Maybe she did.

"Listen, Megan. It's a win-win for you. You get to buy a new house, and I'll pay child support and alimony. The whole shebang. It's everything you wanted, right?"

Silently, she shook her head. "So, what happens next?" she asked, eyeing Amelia who was returning up to the lawn.

"Next, we sign off on this. No mediation is a good thing. It can go straight through. I guess then the divorce can be finalized." His voice dropped off on the last sentence as though it was hard for him to say. Almost, as though he hated to say it at all.

Megan wondered if she hated to hear it, too.

The next thing, he whispered. Like an afterthought. An allowance. "Megan," Brian said. "I'm tired of this, okay? If you don't want to sell, then you can have the house. You can take it all. I just... " His voice broke, and Megan's eyes began to brim with tears. "I just want you to be happy."

Chapter 32—Clara

Clara had never been one to rush out of school after the final bell, much less *before it*, but here she was, on day two of finding her attention indelibly ripped from the only constant in her life.

Instead of asking permission from the principal to leave early yet again, she slipped away twenty seconds before dismissal, scurrying to her car and easing out of the parking lot and toward the house on the harbor. Her sisters weren't expecting her for another fifteen minutes at least, but Clara could not wait. She had to know. She had to be part of the mess, as much as she hated it. Her future—her ability to sculpt out a future for herself—depended on it.

As Clara turned right onto the easement just past Harbor Avenue, she spotted just Megan's vehicle. A sliver of jealousy wedged its way into her chest. The thought of her sisters carpooling around town, sipping mimosas at Fiorillo's, and bouncing in and out of shops in the village with little paper bags of souvenirs made her feel unreasonably angry.

She tried hard to push it aside, focusing instead on what she would say. "I'll take the cottage, if you don't mind." Or maybe: "I'd like to have the cottage, regardless of what I've been left. I won't bother you for anything else. All I want is the cottage." No matter what words she practiced in her head, she sounded like a baby.

Now, Clara turned her attention to the narrow street in front of the house. Just as her eyes focused, a flash of black dashed in front of her car. A squirrel or a bird—no. It was a bigger animal. Not big, but bigger than a bird, for sure. And four-legged.

Slamming her foot on the brake, Clara's heart pounded in her chest. She threw the car into park and tore out of it and around to the front, where she was positive she would find small animal carnage.

A voice cried out from across the street. "He's okay; he's okay!"

Clara glanced up to see an attractive stranger jog toward her. Ignoring him momentarily, she searched the pavement until her eyes landed on a little dog, splayed on its back in submission, his needle-shaped tail wagging like a windshield wiper across the ground.

"Dobi?" Clara asked, bending down and tickling the chubby pup's belly.

"Sorry about that," the man said as he neared. Clara looked up, squinting through the eastern-facing sun behind him.

"Jimmy?" she asked, shielding the rays to make sense of his features.

"At your service." He grinned cockily and joined her on the steaming asphalt.

"I thought I hit him," Clara murmured as she gave Dobi's slick potbelly one final pat before rising and smoothing her dress.

Jimmy hooked the leash clip on the dog's collar and faced the house, gawking in admiration. "Wow. I can't believe you grew up here," he commented, raising his eyebrows to Clara.

She shrugged. "Yeah. I guess."

"Everything okay?" he asked, dipping his chin. "I mean now that we've established Mr. Dobi here is alive to tell the tale of his near-death experience."

Clara began to reply that she was tired, but Jimmy held up a hand, his eyes growing wide.

"Wait, wait. You probably heard, huh?"

"Heard what?" Clara answered quickly, desperate for any crumb of information she could wrap her brain around.

Aloof, Jimmy answered easily. "Well, I mean I just got off the phone with Amelia. She didn't want me to come down here, but things sounded pretty serious, so I figured I'd better check in on all of you girls. This Matt guy seems like he's up to no good."

"Matt?" Clara played dumb as she noticed movement behind one of the windows of the house. "You mean Matt... *Fiorillo*?" she lowered her voice.

"I think so. Yeah, well Kate took the... whatdoyoucallit? The barge? Or ferry or whatever—she took it to his place and then some drama went down, you know. I guess there's a question about him and your mom, maybe? Amelia didn't tell me *everything*, but I put two and two together. This Matt guy, I guess, has lived here forever. He even showed up to your mom's funeral? And then he came to the house earlier today to 'check on things.'" Jimmy threw up air quotes. Clara hated air quotes.

She scrunched her face. "What do you mean Matt and my mom?"

"And *you*," Jimmy replied, pointing an accusatory finger at Clara. "I mean, Matt being your real dad, right? That's the big scandal, right?" Clara felt her face grow hot and her heart thud against her chest wall at Jimmy's words. But he kept talking, stupidly. "Small towns, I tell you. I'm glad I'm from the city. We don't keep anything quiet there. If you have a crazy family, you know about it from *day one*."

***

Clara burst through the front door fuming. "Kate!" She screamed across the foyer and towards the kitchen.

Kate's face appeared in the doorframe. Behind her, Matt Fiorillo.

"Is it true?" Clara wailed, glaring venomously at both of them.

Megan stepped in from the parlor, grabbing Clara's arm before she had a chance to peel off down the hall. "Clara, what is going on?"

"Is *he*... my... my *father*?" Clara pointed her finger at the man.

The reaction that smacked across both Kate's and Matt's faces told her all she needed to know.

Stupid Jimmy, the interloping tourist-boyfriend, was right. She spun around to see him amble in behind her, little Dobi cuddled into his arms. Clara threw a hand back towards him. "He told me *everything*."

Amelia appeared behind Megan, bewilderment on her face.

Clara had no idea what *they* had to be confused about. *They* knew the truth all along. *They* were the secret keepers.

Amelia joined Clara at the door then reached for and grabbed Dobi out of Jimmy's hands. "Whatever you said, get out. Leave," she spat.

Jimmy started to protest, but Megan opened the door and reiterated Amelia's command. "Leave, Jimmy."

He did.

Clara's breathing had slowed only marginally. The leftover breaths now available to her were turning into tears and pricking at the corners of her eyes. "Is it *true*?" she asked everyone and no one, her eyes searching her sisters and avoiding Matt's hardened stare.

She didn't even know Matt. All she knew about Matt Fiorillo was that he was Kate's boyfriend before Clara was even born. She'd rarely seen him around town. Even when she saw his supposed daughter at the funeral, they seemed wholly unfamiliar.

Except for one shadowy memory. Something she hadn't recognized until that very moment. Except in that memory, they were in opposite positions.

She was there, in the kitchen doorway. Matt was where she now stood, in the foyer, looking floppy but cute. Cute for an older guy, Clara distinctly recalled.

He'd shown up one day randomly, when Clara was perhaps ten or so. Her mother greeted him coldly and made him wait in the foyer until she'd retrieved a sweater. After that, they'd left together. Curious, Clara had flown to the windows in the parlor, peeking out and listening hard through the lavender plant that stretched in its pot just beyond the cracked window.

But she hadn't caught any of their conversation. And the only other part of the memory that she now recalled was her mother returning into the house and warning Clara that she had better never talk to that Fiorillo boy ever.

Easy enough for Clara.

She didn't talk to anyone.

Chapter 33—Amelia

Amelia pressed her hand to her heart, willing it to slow down. Jimmy was such an *idiot*. A freaking *idiot*.

He'd gotten it wrong. Almost all wrong. Implying that Clara was the product of some affair between their mom and Matt?

Gross.

And, wrong.

Jimmy and all his false bravado about helping repair the house and enjoying some romantic interlude while they were in town was a hilarious fantasy. Not even a fantasy. A joke. He was a joke! Their relationship was a joke. Especially in contrast to the very real family situation that lay before them now.

She bounced Jimmy from her mind and wrapped a protective arm around Clara. "He doesn't know what he's talking about," she whispered, regretting ever mentioning anything to that halfwit.

"Please," Kate interrupted. "Will everyone give us some privacy?" Amelia's older sister pierced Megan, Amelia, and then Matt each with a glare.

"Okay," Amelia answered, giving Clara one last hug and nodding Megan and Matt through to the back porch.

***

Once they were outside, Amelia couldn't bear the burden of being separated from the secret that Kate was about to reveal inside the house. It was almost painful, the keep-awayness of it all. But the truth was not Amelia's to handle.

Matt blew out a sigh, shoved his hands in his pockets, and—without a word—walked down to the beach, not bothering to glance behind.

Amelia started after him, but Megan interceded. "Let him go, Amelia."

She turned and faced Megan. "Shouldn't he be in there?"

Megan shrugged. "It's not our call. Let's just mind our own business for now. I'm sure Kate will call us in when she's ready."

Amelia set Dobi down in the grass and unhooked his leash. He dashed away, leery enough of the sea wall to stay near.

"I can't stand this," Amelia whispered, stretching her arms in a wide circle above her head. "I can't stand it!"

Megan answered, "Let's get our minds off of it. Talk about something else."

"Like what? What could we possibly have to talk about while they are in there dealing with this?" Amelia drew a dramatic circle around the property, as though it was the pit of the big drama.

"Jimmy, for starters," Megan replied, a tired smile curling her mouth.

"Nothing to talk about there. He made a fool out of himself. Case closed."

"Are you going to break up with him finally?" Megan pressed.

"Are you going to divorce Brian?" Amelia shot back, an attitude edging into her voice, though from where it came was beyond her.

Megan glanced at her phone then clicked it off. Amelia had an opportunity and an instinct, and she went for it, snatching the phone from Megan's hand and turning her back sharply as she turned the screen on and shuffled through Megan's apps as she wailed behind Amelia, clawing her back.

Amelia deftly avoided giving up the device long enough to open the dating app. As she began scrolling through the unfamiliar interface, it occurred to her that Megan had stopped protesting all together. Instead, the younger, darker Hannigan sister now stood a couple of feet away, her arms crossed and her lower lip trembling.

"Megan," Amelia said, her voice low. She dropped the phone and held it out. "I'm sorry. I was just joking. I shouldn't have—"

Megan wiped an errant tear from her cheek and took the phone before tapping quickly and flashing the phone up to Amelia's face. "See?"

Amelia leaned forward and squinted. A digital inbox glowed back at her. She wasn't sure what she was supposed to see, so she shook her head helplessly back.

"Look," Megan pressed the phone back at Amelia, forcing her to take it and study it closer. "I don't know why I'm being weird about it. Just look, if you're so curious."

Four messages fell beneath what appeared to be Megan's "profile," which offered the shadow of a head instead of Megan's photo and a semi-anonymous handle, *meg_2020*.

Amelia glanced up at Megan, whose eyes were now dry and, curiously, even smiled back. A... nervous smile?

"*Mark47* says, 'can i get a pic?'" Amelia read aloud.

Megan lifted an eyebrow and nodded her on.

Amelia went to the next. "*TheBigMichigander* says, 'Hi. How are you?'"

This time, Megan shrugged.

"You didn't answer them," Amelia pointed out, reading on to find that the next two messages were also vague and unreturned. "So, you're testing the water?" Amelia prompted, completely absorbed by the unfolding circumstances despite everything else going on just yards away in the house.

"In a way," Megan replied. She shook her head and rubbed her thumbs beneath her eyes as if to clear the threat of more tears.

"What's going on?" Amelia asked, confused by Megan's veiled hints and moodiness.

A deep sigh lifted Megan's chest. She glanced up at the house then fixed her gaze back on Amelia. "I'm not on that thing to meet men."

Amelia stole another look at the phone, trying to discern something—*anything*. She came up empty. "I don't understand."

"It's embarrassing, I guess. I don't know. I didn't want to say anything until I worked it out."

"So you *are* seeing someone?"

"No," Megan answered, her eyes drifting off until they landed on Matt in the distance. Amelia followed her stare. Sadness tugged at her heart. There were so many answers for them to uncover, and time was of the essence. At least, if Amelia wanted to return to the city in time to resume her waitress gig and prep for Lady Macbeth.

"Then what, Megan? Spell it out, for the love of God. Spell. It. Out."

"I applied to work for them," Megan answered, covering her mouth as she said it.

Amelia frowned. "What?"

"I applied to work for the app. The matchmaking app. Just before Mom's funeral. I haven't heard back yet, but I wanted to get an idea of what it was like. You know?"

"So *that's* it? *That's* what you've been keeping from us?" Amelia laughed.

A sheepish smile took hold of Megan's mouth. "It's... look, I haven't even heard back yet. I don't have the tech skills, probably. And what matchmaking company would hire someone who's in the middle of a divorce?"

Grinning broadly now, Amelia rushed Megan in a hug, burying her face in her sister's shoulder. "I'm so proud of you," she whispered.

Megan laughed in reply. "Your standards must be low. You're proud of me for applying for a *job* and keeping it a secret?"

"No," Amelia replied. "I'm proud of you for following *your dream*."

Chapter 34—Kate

They sat at the table together in silence, the two blonde-haired Hannigans. The house felt bigger, and in it, Kate felt more vulnerable.

She swallowed hard and stared out through the window, watching on as Amelia and Megan pounced on each other in the grass like obnoxious children. Kate envied them. Amelia and Megan had always been safe, removed. Separated and shielded. *Free.*

Not Kate. She was smack dab in the middle of it. Kate was the *cause* of it.

Matt's shape reappeared in the distance. Her heart ached. For him. For *them*. For all the years that had filled up like an ocean. Mostly, Kate's heart ached for Clara, who should have been none the wiser.

Kate thought about the will and wondered what her mother was thinking when she left the house out? And even more than that, why didn't Michael Matuszewski ask?

"I'm not sure how to start," Kate whispered, returning her attention to Clara. It was maybe the first time in years Kate had looked upon her like she did now—*differently*.

Clara's eyes, bright and blue, took on a milky effect. Darkened hollows framed them, adding to her tired face. Her hair, tied back at the top with a barrette, tugged free at her temples in brittle flyaways. Clara's skin, devoid of much makeup, drew down in red splotches along her chin—hormonal acne she was too young to kick.

Kate wondered what it would have been like to have a daughter.

"I just want to know why," Clara replied, taking in a deep breath and letting it out slowly through parted lips.

"Mom didn't mean to leave you out of the will," Kate answered. "She just didn't update it."

"Why didn't she?" Clara shot back, her brows furrowing toward the bridge of her nose.

"You came so much later, and—" Kate stopped short, unwilling to reveal the next thing. The big thing.

"Mom was in Michael Matuszewski's office," Clara responded, her tone pleading, even desperate. "Why wouldn't she think to?"

"Well, in a way she *did* make an adjustment," Kate replied at last, reaching into her purse which sat slumped on the floor.

Clara's face lifted. Hope.

Kate pressed the envelope onto the table beneath her palms, securing it there for the time. "She had a diary, I guess you could say. And she left an entry for us, or me, specifically," Kate said at last, her eyes welling up.

Her eyes widening, Clara shook her head. "A *diary entry*?"

"Yes. She tore it out. Maybe there are other entries, but I'm not sure. It seems like she left this one as part of... her will or something. I think... " A sob escaped Kate's lips. "I think she was confused. But, Clara, she meant well."

Tears streamed down Clara's ruddy cheeks. Her neck blossomed in red patches—evidence of grief and relief and shock.

"But that's not all," Kate whispered.

Clara's crying paused momentarily as she locked eyes with Kate. "Then, what?"

"You," Kate began, her voice trembling uncontrollably against the weight of the truth. "Clara, you… " They looked at each other, and Kate could feel Clara's heart pounding in her own chest wall. Nausea churned in her gut.

"What?" Clara whimpered back.

"Clara, you are not our sister."

Chapter 35—Clara

A panic attack.

Clara was officially experiencing a panic attack. Her entire life flashed before her eyes. Little moments here. Big memories there. Her feeling left out for all her childhood. Her hard work. The cleaning. The life of lonesomeness. Her chest began heaving. Her neck grew tight. No tears. Just panic.

"Calm down. Clara, calm down."

Clara could hear the words, but Kate's face became blurry. Foggy. Like a pencil eraser had been rubbed across her features. "What are you—what are you—" She repeated the same three words over and over again, trying to steady herself against the failing vision and cramping muscles.

Kate rose from her chair and knelt next to Clara, her hands pressed against Clara's cheeks, leveling her jaw. "Clara, shh. Listen to me. Calm down, okay?"

One deep breath later, and Clara could see again. The tears came now. Frightful tears. "What are you talking about, *Kate*," she hissed between sobs.

"Clara, when I was in high school, I got pregnant."

The sobs halted abruptly. Clara *knew* she misheard. Or misunderstood. She sniffled and rubbed her fist beneath her nose, smearing away a mishmash of fluids from her face. "You never told me you had a baby," Clara answered, lamely. How could she not know that her older sister was a teen mom? "What happened?" Clara asked, feeling her heartbeat return to normal.

Kate blinked and frowned but went on, answering in slow, looping words like Clara was a toddler. "Matt and I... " Kate glanced out the window behind her, as if she hoped he'd appear at the door. Clara was glad he didn't. "We were in love. But that's no excuse, I guess. I'd tell you it was a mistake, but I'd be lying. I got pregnant. That's why we went to Arizona. Mom was mortified. She didn't know how to handle it, I guess." Kate stopped, shaking her head. Fresh tears budding along her lower lash line.

"So what did you do with it?"

Kate offered a half smile, wiping away the wetness from her cheeks. "The baby?"

Clara nodded back.

"Well, we didn't know what to do. Mom was so worried about people in town finding out. It was... uncomfortable."

"What about Dad?" Clara asked.

Kate let out a small laugh. "That's the funny thing. He wasn't mad. He was okay with it, I guess. I mean, not *okay* with it. But he just figured we'd deal with it. That's why he started building the cottage."

"What do you mean?"

"Mom figured she could hide me away there. With the baby, I mean. We could keep it a secret."

"Is that what happened? Did you move into the cottage? What happened to the baby?" Clara's panic returned, as she began conducting some simple calculations in her head.

But before she had a chance to finish doing the math, Kate answered, quelling her questions for the moment. "Mom decided to adopt the baby."

Clara's head bobbed and her vision grew blurry again.

Kate grabbed her hands, squeezing them, and whispered through tears, "Clara, *you were the baby.*"

***

The next several minutes were a blur. Clara had already put two and two together in the course of Kate's story. But the confirmation of what she suspected slid across her like an avalanche.

Her panic attack took hold once again, paralyzing her muscles and launching her stomach into full-blown nausea. She rose from her chair and stumbled to the kitchen sink, retching until Kate ran out to the back and hollered for the others to come inside.

Three women rushed in behind Clara as she lifted her head from the porcelain. She turned the faucet on, scooping tap water into her mouth and swishing. It was the most normal thing she could do.

Amelia and Megan twittered behind, shushing her and patting her back. Clara felt Kate's presence nearest her, murmuring assurances and rubbing Clara's neck.

"She must be in shock. Let's have her lie down." The voice, calm and deep, was a stranger's. And, apparently, her father's. Another wave of nausea filled her throat and she heaved again into the sink.

Kate continued rubbing her neck then directed orders to the others. "Get a glass for water. See if there's ice in the freezer. Pack it in a dish towel. Clear the parlor sofa."

It was an emergency. An actual emergency. "Take me to the hospital," Clara wheezed from the sink. "Take me away from here. Away from all of you," she wheezed between heaves. Dramatics be damned, she couldn't handle the pain in her heart.

But the others just kept on shushing her, treating her like the baby she was. The baby she had always been.

***

Minutes later, minutes that felt like hours, Clara lay prone on the sofa, alone now. Dust motes floated past her blank stare and down beneath her slack jaw, settling onto her blouse. A blouse she'd selected for its conservativeness and comfort. The perfect teacher's uniform. Boring and trusty. Just like Clara.

"Clara?" Kate's face appeared, cutting off rays of the setting sun as they pierced the parlor windows and cut across the younger one, allowing for her view of the twirling, whirling dust.

Clara blinked. "What?"

Kate squeezed herself onto the cushion. "Can we talk?"

"I don't know what to say."

"Well," Kate went on, her voice still trembly, "you must have some questions, right? Do you want to go over anything, or—"

At that, Clara tugged the ice-packed dish towel from her forehead and pulled herself to a sitting position. "You're my *mother*." It wasn't a question. Just a statement. But Clara wanted to test out the words. See how they felt. She swallowed and took in Kate's features. Her own features, in many ways. The blonde hair—kept up by highlights nowadays—the blue eyes and petite, aquiline features. Features that were also inherited from Nora. But now, Nora was dead. Her inheritance didn't matter anymore.

Kate nodded silently.

Clara glanced past her, toward the foyer. "Did Matt leave?"

"No. He's waiting."

"For what? To talk to me? Where has he been all these years, Kate? What happened between you two?" For some reason, their relationship felt more pertinent than their parenthood.

"Mom made us end it, of course. Clara, it was a major scandal. It was as big of a deal then as it feels to you now. You know? A shock?"

Clara's face softened. She sat up and crossed her legs beneath her, and Kate moved deeper into the sofa. A stale smell tickled Clara's nose, and she felt a sneeze coming on.

"God bless you," Kate said in reply to Clara's gaped mouth and subsequent spasm.

Clara couldn't help but giggle. Kate smiled.

"Kate, I'm so sorry," she whispered.

"Are you kidding? You have nothing to apologize for. That would be me. I'm the one who ought to say I'm sorry."

"But for what?" Clara answered.

Her older sister—or whoever Kate was to Clara—hesitated for a moment, gathering her thoughts before replying, it appeared. "Clara, I bent to Mom's will very easily. Especially back then. I felt like I didn't have a choice. Coming back here as a mother would have been hard. And, even if I was up to the task, things might have been different for all of us, you know?"

"How?" Clara pressed, desperate to know anything else that would help her paint a truer picture of her childhood—the one that felt so much less like a childhood. If Kate had raised her, would she have had playmates? Would Ben and Will be obnoxious little brothers she shooed away from her bedroom? "Oh," Clara added, upon finishing the thought.

"I would have had nothing to offer you. Matt and I couldn't have made it work, not financially. And... I never would have met Paul, probably." Kate closed her eyes for a moment.

Clara interrupted. "I still can't believe it. It feels... *unreal*." She lifted a hand and pressed it to Kate's arm. Her sister—*her mother*—felt older beneath her fingers. Her skin felt different. She even seemed to smell different. Everything, in the blink of an eye, had changed. "It still doesn't explain the will," Clara said flatly. "If Mom—er, *Nora*, I guess, *adopted* me, then I should still get one-fourth. Just like I always thought. I should still be her daughter, right?"

Kate swallowed hard, her eyebrows falling low and her voice dropping. "I think you need to read the diary entry."

Chapter 36—Nora

December 1992

I lied to my daughters.

There, I've written it. I can't say it. I won't say it. I will never say it.

I was not going to commit to paper the events of the past year. I was dedicated to keeping the secret. Let me be clear: I am still dedicated to this secret. But you know how secrets go! They fester like blisters, desperate for someone to come along and poke at them until they bleed.

I won't let anyone poke, but I have to confess somewhere. To someone.

I did not file the paperwork.

I did not adopt Baby Clara.

Chapter 37—Kate

They were all together, sitting at a large weather-worn table on the back porch, sipping from glasses of lukewarm soda. Two boxes of delivered pizza flapped open and closed to the rhythm of the breeze. Kate studied her glass. It was one of the many she'd known as a child, growing up among the heirlooms left to them in the house on the harbor. Hannigan heirlooms.

Amelia and Megan were the only two with any appetite left, but it was with deference that they nibbled on their slices, chatting quietly to themselves while Matt and Clara cracked open the lengthy process of getting to know each other.

Their words were stilted, to be sure, awkward, even. But Kate saw the flecks of hope in Matt's eyes, flecks she'd seen when she'd first told him she was pregnant. Flecks that died off when Nora had turned him away, time and again, from their door in the days and weeks—and then even years—after the news.

Did Kate and Matt ever meet in secret? No.

They never met again, in fact. It was too painful. That she carried his child when she and Matt were both only children was too much for the teenage girl to bear.

Instead, Kate finished school, graduating quietly among the rest of her class then heading to college where she would meet Paul; safe, dependable Paul. From there, life settled into place, happy distractions cropping up one after another as if to reassure Kate that she had moved on. That she *could* move on.

But Kate Hannigan *never did* move on. Yes, she grew accustomed to knowing Clara as her sister, but it was always and painfully an act, a fact that she had to force herself to digest and learn and apply, much like a newly wedded woman must digest and learn and apply her married name. And yet, Kate wasn't a newly wedded woman, excited to change her name. She was a mother thwarted. Jilted, even.

Now, she knew that that's exactly what Nora had left Kate in her will—a silent inheritance—a jilting.

At first, back when they were still inside on the sofa together, once Clara came around, Kate thought it best that everyone go home and call it a day. They could address the remainder of the estate and the fallout from the news another time, when they'd be better able to handle it.

Clara had protested, however. She had no one to talk to, after all. She needed her *sisters*, she'd claimed.

And that's when they agreed that Wendell Acton had always been right. They could still be sisters. They could leave it alone. Let go and let God.

So, there they sat, Kate, Amelia, Megan, and Clara. Still sisters. Nothing more. Nothing less.

***

After another sleepover in Clara's cramped quarters at The Bungalows, Kate awoke early, much earlier than the others. The predawn morning hummed outside Clara's window.

Kate admired the place. It had the charm of the 1920s and the comfort of living in community among others. She knew that Clara wasn't very social, much like her.

Quietly, she poured herself a chilled glass of water and slipped out onto the back patio and tucked herself onto the wicker seat. The courtyard needed a little work. Flowers. A good raking. But Kate wasn't bothered. She wasn't upset with Clara. She knew that Clara had long been living under a state of oppression, and it was time that she did a better job of helping her.

All three of them could do a better job. So, Kate decided they'd have a final family meeting. At the house on the harbor again, this time without Matt.

Yet, Kate had to see him again. She couldn't sleep the night before. She couldn't move on without some sort of closure... or *something* with Matt.

Nervous, she pulled her phone from her pajama pocket where she'd slipped it first thing when she rolled out of bed.

She moved to her text messages and shuffled into her exchange with Matt. So far in the past day, their messages were terse and business oriented.

It was early, very early, but she couldn't wait. And if it woke him, oh well. Tapping out another terse, brief message, Kate asked if Matt could meet her and hit send, drawing her finger to her mouth and nibbling on a sharp hangnail as she slid the phone back into her pocket.

Mentally, she began preparing for the meeting they would have as sisters. The "Who Gets What" meeting that had been dangling over them for going on two weeks now, in effect. Kate had a sense of what she'd like to see happen, but then again it was not quite her place to dictate the matter.

A vibration tickled her thigh. Like a cowgirl, Kate whipped the phone out and held the screen to her face.

Matt.

Her heart skipped a beat.

She tapped the message open and read and reread his words. He hadn't slept either. He'd love to meet. She could name the place and time, and he would be there.

Swallowing, she responded with the location and the time. *The house on the harbor. Now.*

***

There were no ferries, but Matt had a boat. He could have docked it at the house, if the Hannigan dock were in any decent shape, which it was not.

Once Kate arrived at the house, she immediately regretted it. Thinking that, instead, she could have walked to the marina.

Hesitating at the front door, it occurred to her that she still had time. She could walk there. Surprise him. Then, they could walk back to the house—or even wherever they wanted to go. Anywhere in Birch Harbor.

She spun on a heel and, for the first time in a long time, followed her heart instead of her brain.

Morning was settling over the harbor, and the warm glow of the sun thawed Kate's hardness. A smile even pulled at her face when she saw Matt, there at his slip, tying off his boat and carousing with the few others who were on the dock so early.

It was hard to avoid drinking in the sight of him. Khaki shorts gave way to tanned, taut calves. His polo hung loose around his torso, but with each jerk of the rope, his shoulder blades cut through the light fabric, revealing a fit upper half.

Kate tucked a strand of her hair behind her ear and ran her tongue across her lips. She'd been limited in primping, but she felt good about herself. Healthy. Plain but pretty. It's how she felt when she was in Birch Harbor. Like herself.

She felt like a spy, watching him from a close distance without his consent. But then, as he strode up the dock, his sun-kissed face turning away from the men he'd just waved to, he saw her.

A broad grin spread across his face. Kate thought she saw the shape of her name part his lips.

"Matt," she whispered, slowly striding toward him. "Hi," she said once they met on the sidewalk that would carry them up and down Harbor Avenue.

"Hi," he replied, scratching the back of his head, his hair flopping over his forehead in a boyish mop. "Good morning," he added, smiling again.

"Good morning. Thanks for meeting me."

"How's Clara?" His face turned solemn and he dipped his chin, searching her eyes for a good answer. The right answer.

But there was no right or wrong anymore. Not since the truth came out. There was only *now*. "We talked a lot last night," she answered him. "She's... hurt. She doesn't understand why we never told her. I'm starting to wonder the same thing myself."

He nodded then said, "Let's go for a walk, okay?" She agreed and they strode side by side in the direction of the house on the harbor. "You know, Kate," he went on. "Lots of families have secrets. Some of them are way worse than yours."

Intrigued by his attempt to reassure her, Kate glanced Matt's way. "Oh yeah? Do the Fiorillos have skeletons in their closets, too?"

Chuckling, he replied, "Maybe. Well, yes. I do. My family doesn't know about Clara, for one. Not even Viviana." He slowed to a stop and licked his lips, his hands shoved deep in his pockets.

Frowning, Kate stopped too and faced him. "I'm sorry," she said. "I'm sorry about that."

Matt shrugged half-heartedly. "Can I tell them now?"

Caught off guard by this, she blinked. "Do you *want* to?"

He pushed air out of his mouth and shook his head. "It's *all* I've wanted to do. Do you know how hard it is to live in the same town as your daughter and never... " He faltered, searching for words that she could have filled in for him.

And, she did. "You mean do I know hard it is to live in the same *house* as your daughter and be forced to pretend that I didn't give birth to her? Why, yes. I know that feeling quite well."

Matt flushed a deep red, his jaw working as he licked his lip and twisted his head side to side slowly, uncomfortably. "Kate," he whispered, pulling his hands from his pockets and running his fingers through his hair before pinning her with a sad look. "I'm sorry. I didn't mean—"

"It's fine," she replied, compassion filling her voice. "I shouldn't have thrown it back in your face like that." She regretted being harsh with him. Swallowing, she jutted her chin back up the road. He took her cue and they resumed their stroll. "I guess we both know what it feels like."

"You're the one who carried her," he pointed out.

"You're the one who stayed here," she shot back as they neared the house.

Matt's eyebrows drew together above the bridge of his nose and, catching her entirely by surprise, he grabbed Kate's hand in his and squeezed it hard. They now stood on the other side of the stout, white fence. Kate suddenly couldn't tell if she was fifteen again or not.

He cleared his throat. "Are *you* going to stay this time, Kate?"

She fell away from him half a step, dizziness clouding her vision. It was a thought she'd considered for some time. Returning to Birch Harbor. To her sisters.

To... Matt?

"I'm not sure," she answered, finding her footing and straightening. "Maybe. I don't know what we're doing with the properties." As she said it, she remembered his initial interest. The notion of Matt Fiorillo buying her family home had felt sour before, but now it didn't. Now, it made sense. It was a way for him to connect with Clara. And, with Kate. "Did you... did you still want to buy this?" She waved a hand up at the towering home.

He shook his head. "I don't think so. I have other projects going on, and I'm away from Vivi enough. Mostly, I was curious. I figured I'd see what you all planned to do. What would happen, you know?"

"Matt," Kate asked, crossing her arms over her chest. "Did you know that our mom was going to reveal the secret or something? Is that why you poked your head in?" She said it with a smile, but the accusation hung in the morning air like a missile.

"No, no, no." Matt held his hands up in defense. "I never knew she'd tell you. I figured she *wouldn't*. Your *dad* on the other hand... "

Kate's eyes grew wide. "What do you mean my *dad*?"

He muttered a swear and bit down on his lower lip. "Listen, no. I mean, I took your dad as the type who might have said something. I tried to talk to both of them, Kate. When you were in Arizona, I went to your dad. But he didn't know what to say to me. That's the impression I got. He was confused, I guess. He didn't know how to handle the whole thing. Especially your mom."

Propping her hands on her hips, Kate frowned. "He didn't know how to handle my mom?"

"Yeah, I mean... your dad was a nice guy. I didn't want to come between them or interfere with the 'plan,'" he threw up air quotes.

"What 'plan?'" Kate mimicked him.

"To keep your secret. To keep the town from knowing that Nora Hannigan's daughter got pregnant by some Italian kid." He laughed nervously.

Kate frowned. "You think my parents didn't like your family?"

Matt blew out a sigh, rubbing his eyes with his fists. "Your mom didn't like that you got pregnant. And I'm the one who did that to you. I think she saw me as a... perpetrator or something. The bad guy."

Shaking her head, Kate replied, "She didn't think you were a bad guy. She thought I was an embarrassment."

"It was a hard thing," Matt agreed at last. "Your dad went easy on me though. I remember coming here" he lifted his chin up to the house. "I knocked. I was so nervous about what he'd say. If he'd punch me in the face or what. But he wasn't even home. I ran into him at the hardware store a day later and he shook my hand and *apologized.* He *apologized*, Kate."

"Why?" she asked, her face crumpling at the memory Matt offered. The memory someone had of her father. The father who left them in the midst of their tragedy, never to be heard from again. His whole existence and disappearance shrouded in some horrid small-town mystery.

"I'm not sure. He just said he felt bad about how things were unfolding. He said he knew what I was going through. But you know what else he said?"

"What?" she whispered, a breeze brushing her hair across her face.

"He told me not to give up."

A sob escaped Kate's mouth and her shoulders rounded in. He caught her and pulled her into him, holding her tightly in place. Keeping her together.

She felt Matt's lips press against her head, and she took him in and everything he said. That her father was rooting for them. That her father was the sort of guy who would have loved Kate no matter what happened. That whatever happened to Wendell Acton was not a reflection of Kate's pregnancy or Clara's birth.

And, she realized that Matt made good on his word.

He hadn't given up, and he never would.

"I'm going to stay, too," she murmured into his neck.

Matt gently pushed her away, searching her face earnestly. "In Birch Harbor?" he asked.

Fresh tears dried along her cheeks as she nodded. "Yes. Somewhere here. In Birch Harbor. Near Clara. Near *you*."

Chapter 38—Clara

After coffee, Amelia, Megan and Clara walked down the road to meet Kate at the house. Wednesdays were late starts for teaching planning and meetings, but Clara had nothing scheduled, and so it was her prerogative to spend the morning tending to her family business.

Kate had texted that she was meeting Matt. Their reunion felt odd to Clara, but she was glad they might come to some sort of resolution. Closure, maybe.

Then again, closure wasn't exactly the result when someone broke open a long-held secret. In fact, quite the opposite. Now that Clara knew what she knew, they all needed a fresh start. A place to begin again, rather than a place to end.

A safe place.

Itching to get out of the apartment and away from her sisters, Clara nearly asked to spend the morning alone. But that wouldn't do. She was torn between needing privacy and support. Mostly, she wanted answers. Always the planner, Clara needed to know *what would happen next*.

They walked in silence. Amelia and Megan offered their respect by withholding their casual observations and general flightiness.

Once to the house, Clara's stomach churned in unrest.

She glanced around, attempting to locate evidence that Kate and Matt had engaged in some sort of indecency there. It was all she could picture: the woman formerly known as her sister with the man formerly known as a stranger. But once the trio passed through the gate and headed toward the house,

Kate appeared in its doorway, alone, her face awash in morning light.

"Let's grab breakfast. I think we'll handle this better with a healthy dose of carbs by the dock. Sound good?" Kate was all but beaming. It was hard not to catch her happiness, even in light of the hard days behind them.

Amelia and Megan looked at Clara, clearly deferring to her judgment. She grinned back. "Sounds great."

***

"Do we need the lawyer here?" Amelia asked, lifting an eyebrow at the others as they sipped on fresh brewed coffee from the deli while awaiting their toasted bagels.

Clara looked at Kate for the answer. The latter lifted her shoulders. "I think we need to decide who wants what, first. Then, we can take that to Michael and contest the estate. Or, if we can all agree on something else, then maybe... oh, jeez. I really don't know."

Clara was hoping to save time where she could in order to make it to first period on time. "I printed these out," she said, passing around a neat page that listed each property, the items indicated by the will, and other significant mementos she'd like to address.

The others took a minute to study her handout.

Finally, Megan lifted her head. "The biggest thing is the house on the harbor. It's not in the will, so it should be liquidated and split among the three of us, technically. But if we contest, we split the proceeds among all four. We can still contest, right, Kate? On the grounds that we were under the belief that Clara was adopted?" Megan didn't mince words, and Clara found herself to be glad of that.

Kate nodded. "From what I read online, we can contest and might have a case. The diary entry would be proof, and Michael himself was witness to it. Plus, Matt can testify—is that the right word? Well, he can *testify* that he signed off on some document about giving up parental rights just like I did. We didn't know she never took those documents anywhere. We didn't know that she shredded them up, or whatever. We were just kids."

"Right," Amelia replied, taking a deep breath.

The bagels arrived, but each woman set hers aside in favor of the business at hand.

"So, do we sell the house on the harbor?" Megan asked again, this time eyeing each sister in turn.

Amelia shrugged.

Clara swallowed.

Kate answered, "No. I don't think so. I know it needs some work, but there's too much history there. We have to keep it."

"Who's going to take care of it?" Megan asked.

Kate lifted a hand. "I will. I'll take care of it."

"You don't live here, Kate," Amelia reasoned. "It'll just fall to Clara again."

A thin line formed on Clara's mouth. "I'm sorry," she interjected defensively.

"No, no," Amelia replied. "I don't mean to say you can't handle it. I mean it's not fair that we always default to you. It's time you get your way a little here, girl. We all agree that you've been Mom's punching bag for way too long. Don't you see that, too?"

Warmth flooded Clara's chest, and she nodded. "Yes. Actually, yes. I think I'd like to have my way." A small laugh followed, and Kate reached over and squeezed her shoulder.

"Okay then. So, Kate. If you don't live here, we need to seriously consider another option. I mean if I were to move back to Birch Harbor—which I'm not—I wouldn't want it. It's huge and *so* not me."

"You're thinking about moving back here, aren't you?" Megan deadpanned.

Amelia seemed to hem and haw, finally throwing her hands up. "I don't know! Maybe. But even if I do. I won't live there. Too creepy." She looked past them towards the house on the harbor.

"Megan," Clara said, "you like creepy stuff. Do you want the house?"

Megan shook her head. "No. I want to downsize, if anything. You know, simplify. Streamline. All that."

"Then?" Clara replied, looking at Kate, finally.

"I'll take it." Kate said at last. "I'll take care of it. I'll move here, and I'll take care of it."

The three others glanced at each other.

Megan spoke first. "But how do we split it evenly, then?"

Kate cleared her throat, an answer already appearing to form on her tongue. Clara leaned forward.

"Mom left one property for each of the three of us, right? The Bungalows, the farmland, and the cottage. And now, we have the house on the harbor to split. I think each of us gets one property. The house is easily the most valuable. We can discuss ways for me to pay each of you out. The Bungalows brings in income, though. The farmland, of course, is undeveloped.

We might have to get creative, but a starting point is to assign a property to each one of us."

A silence filled the table. Clara looked down, furrowing her eyebrows nervously as she picked the skin around her nails. She wasn't included in the will. She was at their mercy.

"I think Clara picks first," Megan said at last.

The other three whipped their heads to Megan.

Amelia nodded slowly, her eyes lighting up. "Clara has had the short end of the stick all of her life. She had to deal with Mom alone the longest. And she has had to deal with the trauma of being left out. I agree. Clara picks first."

Clara's heart pounded against her chest wall. Her cheeks felt warm. She began bobbing her knee up and down beneath the table as she looked at Kate.

Kate smiled. "That works for me. Clara, what do *you* want?"

After a beat, Clara answered, "I'd like to have the cottage, if that's okay?"

She glanced around. Something passed between Amelia and Megan, something unreadable.

Kate cleared her throat. "I'm fine with that. What about you two?"

Amelia licked her lips. Megan looked away then back.

"I'll take the land, then," Amelia replied, furrowing her brow.

"What are you going to do with farmland?" Megan asked, scoffing.

"What is any one of us going to do with anything? That's the real question," Kate piped in.

Amelia answered, "Are you getting the house or is Brian? I feel like that's relevant here."

Megan winced and took a sip of her coffee. "I don't technically need a place to live. Brian said I can have the house if I want it. Either that or we sell and split the profits. Kind of like in this scenario."

Clara cringed. It was starting to feel like life was a series of transactions. Negotiations. Agreements where two or more people split a candy bar in half down the middle. But when they got to see their half, it was less than they wanted to begin with. So, no one really got their way.

"Sorry, Megan," Clara whispered. "I bet that's hard."

Megan shrugged. "Yeah. It is. I'm not sure what to do. Either way, you can have the cottage, Clara. You deserve it." Megan reached across the table and covered Clara's hand in hers.

Kate broke in. "What about The Bungalows? Megan, would you want them? Then you have a place to stay, you know, if you need one?"

Megan shook her head. "I'm not a fix-it-upper type. I'm more like Clara that way." She winked at Clara, who was starting to wonder if her "sisters" weren't as distant as she'd always known them to be. Were they acting more like aunts? Had they always acted like aunts? Clara shook the thought, instead focusing on what she knew to be true: they were sisters. Always had been. Always would be.

"How about you, Amelia? You might be good at being a landlady," Kate suggested.

Amelia flashed a smile. "I've got Lady Macbeth," she replied, lifting her palms and her shoulders in a flourish.

"Do you?" Megan asked.

"Well, I certainly hope so. And if I don't, then... "

"Then what?" This time it was Clara who pressed. Clara looked up to Amelia, often enamored of and amazed by her flawless people skills. Her aptitude with audiences and her boisterous, pleasant demeanor at any hour of the day or night.

Amelia considered Clara's question, pressing a finger to her lips and thinking. "If I don't get the role, then I don't know what I'll do. But it won't be living in a four-plex, patching drywall and planting flowers. That's not me," she answered at last.

"Okay," Kate reasoned. "No one has to live there I guess... "

"Wait a minute," Amelia interjected, her eyes lighting up. The others looked at her with hesitant interest. "I... if it comes down to who is getting what, well then... I might like to have a place to stay when I come here, you know?"

"So you want to have a unit available for you as a, what? Vacation rental?" Megan asked, throwing a sidelong glance at Amelia.

Amelia started to protest but Kate shushed her, waving her hand over the food. "Wait a second, wait a second. That's a great idea. We *should* all have a place to stay when we visit. Or, I guess when *you* visit, since it seems Clara and I will be locals." She lifted one corner of her mouth conspiratorially at Clara, who was a little lost. Clara was content to host any of her sisters wherever she lived. Why add a complication?

Kate continued. "We have enough property to offer something more. We could become a business in town. We could have space for Amelia and Megan, and Ben and Will, and Sarah... even Jimmy if we ever decide to let him come back," she added as a joke.

But the others didn't laugh. Their eyes widened at the prospect. A Hannigan sister enterprise. Clara could see the idea percolating in their eyes. Still, Clara didn't want any part of it, really.

"I'm not sure. I don't think I'd make much of a hostess," she offered lamely.

"You've got the cottage. You can just stick to that. But what if... what if Amelia, you take The Bungalows. It can pay for you to keep—to keep doing whatever it is you're doing in New York. I can help manage it here, and you can come to town when you're free to work on more major issues. It'd be a great project for you," Kate added in a sing-song voice.

Megan and Kate exchanged a knowing look, and Clara had the distinct feeling they were in cahoots on something, though what, she did not know.

Amelia frowned and chewed on a nail before replying. "How about this, if I don't get Lady Macbeth, then I'll take The Bungalows. It can be my consolation prize. I'll get to quit The Bread Basket, maybe. It could work," she said, a wry smile crossing her face.

"And Megan, what about you?" Clara offered, worried that things weren't turning out as fair.

"I'll take the land. Worst case scenario, I can sell it for a little profit. But it sounds like Brian is going to be more flexible than I first thought."

"Well," Kate jumped in. "I have an idea that will help all of us moneywise. Separate from The Bungalows' rental income."

"Okay?" Clara asked, feeling outside of their plan still.

"The house on the harbor. We can open a bed and breakfast. I'll run it. I'll keep a room open for whenever you two come to town—or anyone else we want to put up."

"Are you sure?" Megan asked.

Amelia echoed the sentiment. "That's a lot to offer, Kate. Is this all as fair and square as we'd like?"

"Clara gets the cottage and is relieved of her property management duties. I get the house and turn it into an... an inn! And share profits. They won't be much, so don't get too excited. The Bungalows, that's the only piece of the puzzle that's missing. It's a lot of work for me to take that on without getting paid... "

Clara let out a sigh. Nothing felt manageable—*or* fair, she realized. She needed to step up and help. "I don't need the cottage yet. I can stay at The Bungalows for as long as it takes to settle this," she offered helpfully.

Amelia smiled at her, but her face quickly fell into a frown.

"What's wrong?" Clara asked.

Setting her bagel down, she tugged her phone free from her purse. "My phone is buzzing. If it's Jimmy, I swear I'm going—" She stopped abruptly, her frown deepening as she studied the caller ID.

Clara stared on, but Kate rustled next to her, digging her phone out, too. Kate whispered to Clara, "Oh crap, look. I missed a call from Michael."

After briefly glancing at Kate's phone, Clara turned her attention to Amelia, who was now talking to someone in hushed, serious tones.

A moment later she hung up, her eyes flashing across the table. “It was the lawyer. Michael. He tried to call you, Kate,” she fumbled a little, nervous for some reason.

“I know. I missed it. What did he say?” Kate pressed.

“He says there’s something he needs to discuss with us. There’s been a... an oversight.”

Chapter 39—Kate

"I'm terribly sorry. Terribly sorry. I don't know how this slipped by." Sharon stood in Michael's office, wringing her hands safely behind the protection of her receptionist's desk.

Michael, with his hands shoved in his pockets, faced the four of them in the waiting area.

"It's nothing legal. Nothing that can formally alter the conditions of the will like a contesting of the will," Michael warned them, his voice even. "I expect you'll still contest on Clara's behalf, correct?"

Kate waved a hand. "Yes, but... well, there's been an oversight there, too," she admitted, glancing at her sisters.

He cocked his head. "How so?"

Wondering if she should start or if she should press him to reveal his news, she looked to the others for help.

Amelia cleared her throat. "You go first, Michael."

He reached toward Sharon who fussed herself nearly into a fit, grabbing a generic yellow legal envelope. "Here. I just can't imagine the confusion you've suffered," she whined, her attention squarely on Clara.

Michael accepted the envelope and reached his hand inside. "You see, your mother left *four* notes, not just one." He winced a little as he said it and read over each page. "Won't you come back?"

Anxious now, and even excited, Kate motioned her sisters, and they followed Michael to his office, where just a couple days ago they'd first met as one big group. So much had seemed to happen in the interim. Stress and strife. Anxiety and the depths of pain and confusion.

And there was always the answer, there in the darn lawyer's office.

Then again, Kate felt certain that nothing they were about to see would rival the news from her own note.

"Honestly," Michael began, smoothing his tie as he lowered into his seat. "What happened was that Nora had left that yellow envelope with Sharon about a year ago. Apparently, your mother told Sharon to add the contents to her will without reading what was inside. You see," Michael shifted in his seat and cleared his throat.

Kate felt her hands gripping the arms of the chair unnecessarily. It was just paper. Just a note. Surely, there would be nothing *else* to say?

"You see," Michael repeated, fixing his stare on the envelope in his hand. "Sharon had removed just the one page—the one I gave you, Kate," he flicked a glance to Kate. "Since your mom never saw me or asked to open her estate and formally publish a revision, I figured it was a personal note that could be read by you," he looked at her again before his gaze wandered to the others.

They all nodded eagerly, desperate for what was to come.

"Before she threw out the envelope, Sharon dug inside and found three more notes, or pages, what you will." With that, he finally slid his hand out and with it, just as he'd claimed, three more pages—identical to the one Kate had read for herself. Her pulse slowed, and her jaw fell slack. Something like disappointment curled around her heart, but she pushed that down in order to tend to her excitement at what else could be lurking in their mother's private notes. Michael cleared his throat again. "Sharon had forgotten to give the other ones to me, because I was out of the office the day she found them. Well, today she happened to sort through her files and found them again." Michael passed the thin stack to Kate.

Not a single one was addressed to any of them, and no added notes appeared anywhere.

Kate swallowed and looked down the line of her sisters. "Here," she said, handing one page to each sister to read. Kate figured she'd had her own. Now it was their turn.

Forcing patience upon herself, she simply studied each sister, waiting. Waiting. Waiting for an expression of shock or heartbreak or realization, maybe.

Megan lifted her eyes first. "It's another diary entry all right," Megan declared. "Here, listen."

***

May 24, 1973

I didn't think I'd be back here, writing in you. I figured my diary days ended when I was a teenager.

You'll be interested to know I've met someone. Well, I didn't just "meet" him. I was set up on a date, if you can believe that! You turn 24 and people start to wonder about you, I suppose. Yes, my mother arranged for me to have a picnic with Wendell Acton. His family is from Birch Harbor, too. But they keep to themselves. Wendell went to the Catholic school, not Birch Harbor High. I've seen him at church but nowhere else, really. His father runs the lighthouse up north of town. They're a little odd, but that's okay with me.

So, the picnic. Let me tell you about the picnic. It was pretty well perfect. We set out on the lake in Wendell's wooden boat, and he brought sandwiches and a thermos of cider to share. I have to confess, I figured I'd never meet a man I could tolerate.

Boy, can I tolerate Wendell. More than tolerate, in fact.

The real question is, how did my own mother figure Wendell for me? He isn't the sort she would have "pinned" for a daughter of hers. I'm not sure my father knows. Either way, supposedly she bumped into him when he was oiling the pews in the parish hall, and one thing led to another, and there I was, in a wooden row-boat on Lake Huron with this poor boy from the outskirts of town. It was like a scene from a storybook.

When we got back to land, we went for a walk into the woods. He held my hand. I'll never forget this, but we saw fireflies! Yes! The first of the season, right there in this little clearing.

And then, he asked me then and there to be his girlfriend. He said the fireflies were a "sign." I believe in signs, so I had to say yes.

Now here I am, a twenty-something with a beau. We'll see where this goes. Stay tuned!

***

Megan dropped the sheet to her lap, tears wedging themselves into the corners of her eyes. "Did she ever tell us how they met?"

Kate shook her head. "Not that I remember. That's so sweet. She wanted us to have that." Each of them, now, was dabbing at their eyes over the innocent words of their mother. Words that had nothing to do with the will, but that she had to share with them, somehow, even in the throes of her disease.

"Did she tell Sharon why she dropped these off?" Kate asked Michael, gesturing to the other women and their pages.

He shook his head and lifted his palms. "I'm sorry, I don't think so. She was a little... a little confused, if memory serves."

A sadness washed over Kate, but she pushed it down, lifting her chin to Clara, instead.

"What does yours say, Clara?"

The youngest, who'd long ago begrudgingly called into work and requested sub coverage, cleared her throat. "This one seems more recent but there's no date, just a month. It seems like she was trying to... plan ahead or change the will. It's confusing. You're right, Michael. She seems... confused." Clara licked her lips and read through a trembling voice.

***

April

I'm planning to visit the law offices today to make some changes and plans for the future. I don't know the law, and there's a good chance Clara will be left out entirely if I don't give them this here note that I'm writing.

Legally, no, I guess Clara is supposed to get nothing. Oh, the ways of the world. A girl cares for you and loves you and calls you mother and that means nothing to the powers that be.

Well, here I am to tell you, Mr. Lawyer, that you can rewrite the law. Give Clara whatever she wants. She can decide, okay? She's spent her whole life without that chance. I'm even the one to suggest she get her teaching credentials, after all.

Okay, now that we have that squared away, I'd like to add some other provisions. Please change it so the girls can't sell off the properties. I'd like to see them keep the four-plex as rental income. And they can build on the land and have a new home here. Maybe one of the girls needs a fresh start and I'm too busy to see which. Well whoever that is, grant it.

The harbor house must remain as it IS. But for the love of all things holy, don't turn it into a museum. I'd be humiliated to have people rummaging around in my childhood home like no one ever really lived there. That's what happens to these "homes" that turn into museums, you see. The visitors forget what they were truly meant to be. The House on the Harbor was meant to be slept in. With beds and a fridge full of food and a sink full of dishes. I'd have stayed there to keep it alive if it weren't for Wendell leaving us. After a while, a woman can't bear to live with her husband's ghost. So that's why I left for the cottage. I need privacy. I needed to be away from that burden and from the prying eyes of other people who carried their suppositions and held them over my head.

So I left that house.

But you better not, Hannigan girls.

Keep it occupied, dear girls. Please and THANK YOU!

That's not to say I like the idea of a museum, just not MY house.

One other item of business then I'll end. Matt Fiorillo came by the cottage yesterday. Truth be told that's why I decided to make this change at all. He asked me what would become of Clara, if you can believe that. Well, I suppose I can. Matt may be the boy who threw my life into chaos, but he's a good boy. He loves Clara, and he doesn't even know her. I suppose that means something.

So, anyway, here I am, at the behest of that meddling Matt Fiorillo, rewriting my will. I already did, though! I met that other lawyer, the one who left town, and I told him please be sure ALL OF MY DAUGHTERS are IN MY WILL!!! It was a big job, because I didn't have time to go over names and socials. He had to look it up himself. Who can trust these lawyers? Not me. So that's why I've penned this ADDENDUM. To see to it that my girls get their comeuppance, no thanks to you, MATT FIORILLO for your snarky suggestion.

***

Kate belted out a laugh at the final sentence. "I'm sorry," she said through tears. "I can't help it, but she never did like Matt. And only because of the pregnancy. She thought he did it on purpose or something." After a sniffle, Kate added, "It sounds like Mom was more confused than we realized."

Clara, Megan, and Amelia were weeping, but a few laughs made their way through. "It sounds like Matt wanted me to get something," Clara said at last, staring at Kate for an answer.

Kate nodded, shutting her eyes briefly and wiping the rest of the wetness from her cheeks. "Of course he did. He's always loved you, Clara. Even when he couldn't show you."

Warmth seemed to return to Clara's cheeks, and Kate knew in that moment that it was all Clara needed. That slip of paper wrought by their mother's well-meaning hand. It was all the little one needed to feel safe in her family.

And, the note provided some more guidance. A plea from beyond the grave that would help them nail down everything they were struggling with.

"It sounds like our plan is on track with what Mom wanted," Kate pointed out, as the others composed themselves. Michael kept quiet, a soft smile filling his face.

"What is your plan?" he asked quietly.

"For starters, it seems like we need to fill that big heirloom on the harbor with people, don't you think, girls?" Kate asked her sisters, wondering if they agreed.

Each one nodded enthusiastically, but it was Clara who answered. "That's it!" she cried out. "The Heirloom on the Harbor!"

"What do you mean?" Megan asked.

Clara nodded excitedly, but Kate caught on fast. "What about... *The Heirloom Inn*?"

Chapter 40—Amelia

After they'd settled on the name and even began twittering about with a plan—Kate moving back and acting as innkeeper, Clara pitching in after school, Megan joining on the weekends and maybe even bringing Sarah along to help with little repairs and painting projects—Amelia had an idea.

"We could hire Jimmy, you know," she suggested, her face clear and hopeful, but her heart held hostage by *something*. Their reaction?

No.

Her own dreams?

Maybe.

"Over my dead body," Clara declared, crossing her arms over her chest.

Amelia flushed. "We could tell him exactly what to do," she added weakly.

Kate gave her a stern look. "If there's one thing we have all learned this week, it's that Jimmy is a problem, not a solution."

Sighing deeply, Amelia couldn't help but flick a glance to Michael. Talking about Jimmy in his presence felt... perverse, somehow. Like there was a matter of loyalty, and to even mention Jimmy's name was a sin.

A buzz tickled her leg. Thankful for any distraction, Amelia reached down into her purse to check who the text or call was from.

It was a text. From her agent. Rather, Mia, who was her pseudo agent. And friend.

"Oh my God," Amelia whispered.

"What?" Kate asked. "What is it?"

Amelia looked up, embarrassed. Humiliated. Horrified.

"Is everything okay?" Michael asked.

Willing herself not to totally lose it in front of him, she simply shook her head. "I didn't get Lady Macbeth."

Silence came in reply. Kate, who sat next to her, rubbed Amelia's back and pulled her in for a hug.

Megan uttered a quiet apology. Clara did the same.

Michael, the handsome, aloof lawyer, broke the silence. "Were you auditioning for a part in New York?"

Amelia could have sworn she heard something in voice. Was he... impressed?

She nodded to him, lamely.

"I'm sorry to hear. I actually sponsor our community theatre here in Birch Harbor. The Birch Players."

Whipping her head to him, she replied, "What? There was no community theatre when I lived here."

Amelia caught Clara's eyes light up, as she added, "Yes, there is. Some of our kids from the high school are involved in their productions. I think our drama teacher is the one who founded it."

Weakening at the news, Amelia overcame the urge to cry. "That's... cool."

"If you ever move back here, I can connect you," Michael offered. It was a curious thing to offer, in light of Amelia's own sister claiming a solid connection to the company of thespians.

She met his gaze, and a smile formed on her lips. He seemed to grow red, and Amelia smiled broader. "Thank you. Maybe we can... maybe we can exchange phone numbers?"

He nodded dutifully then cleared his throat.

Kate broke up their moment. "Amelia, the paper. Mom's diary entry. What does *yours* say?"

It was the briefest of the notes, and, initially, Amelia wondered why Nora Hannigan had left it at all.

But as her eyes danced over the words and her lips formed full sentences aloud, she came to life with the information.

An adventure.

A project.

***

April

I had a thought today, but I'm not sure if I'll have time to find the answer. It's a big project, and it demands someone who is willing to go on a bit of an adventure—someone who isn't afraid of a project.

I never did find the deed to the lighthouse. In case I don't get to it, please have one of the girls go search for it.

As far as I know, it's part of their inheritance. The lighthouse on the lake, that is.

***

Amelia's eyes flashed up at her sisters and at Michael.

No one knew what to make of it.

"The *lighthouse*?" Kate asked, perplexed.

Amelia shrugged. "It was the Acton's, right? It belonged to Dad's parents."

"And it's where Dad stayed when we went to Arizona," Megan added.

Silence spread between the three of them. Amelia frowned. They'd arrived at so many answers in such a short span of time. Megan and her peculiar obsession with her phone. The mystery of whether Amelia would be the next Lady Macbeth. Hah.

Clara's absence from the will was the most tragic. The most upsetting. Clearly, poor Nora was in worse shape than any of them knew, and the associate Michael had hired back whenever Nora had gone in to make and adjustment wasn't able to offer much help. That besides, Sharon the receptionist was all but useless. Sweet, but useless. Fortunately, the solution was at hand.

"How will this affect our plan?" Megan asked, reading Amelia's mind.

Kate answered, "It doesn't. We're going to tackle the house on the harbor together. After that, we can start chipping away at the other properties. I'll take over on managing The Bungalows. If everyone agrees, still, Clara can help me start clearing the cottage, too. And then she can move in eventually." Kate dipped her chin and looked at Michael. "Maybe you can help us make sure that's on the up and up?"

He nodded, his face serious.

Clara glanced around, nibbling on her lower lip nervously.

Megan and Amelia patted her hands on either side of her, and Amelia whispered, "The cottage is yours. We can start dealing with the other properties. *Together*."

A smile spread around the four women. Peace, at last. After a lifetime of tepid sisterhood made more complicated by a cut-throat, domineering mother, they shared a realization in that moment. Nora wasn't trying to be some evil queen. She was tending to a secret, and that secret nearly broke her, so much so that she tried to pick it open. She tried to set things right.

She was just a little too late.

Amelia felt a sob climb up her throat despite the new, tranquil energy. Or maybe, because of it.

Michael cleared his throat. "I don't want to overstep my boundaries, here, but... I can start looking into the lighthouse, if you four would like?"

Kate let out a sigh. "It's a big project," she answered, her smile fading as she stared across her sisters. "As far as we know, our father still has a claim to it. Wherever he is."

"I could help," Amelia offered, the lump in her throat sliding back down. She winked at Megan, lifted her dark hair off her neck, rolled her shoulders back and stared directly at Michael. "No boyfriend. No Lady Macbeth. I think I could use a *project*."

***

Find out what happens in Birch Harbor next. Order *The Lighthouse* today.

Other Titles by Elizabeth Bromke

Birch Harbor:
Lighthouse on the Lake
Hickory Grove:
The Schoolhouse
The Christmas House
The Farmhouse
The Innkeeper's House
Maplewood:
Christmas on Maplewood Mountain
Return to Maplewood
Missing in Maplewood
The Billionaire's Mountain Bride
The Ranger's Mountain Bride
The Cowboy's Mountain Bride

Acknowledgements

House on the Harbor was a joy to write and largely because of the wonderful people who lent their expertise. Lori Clarey, thank you so much for painting a picture of Pinconning and Tawas and Michigan in general. I love that we are coworkers in more ways than one, now!

From my early childhood into my early adulthood, I spent many summers in the suburbs of Detroit on up through to Frankenmuth and Mackinac. They are some of my fondest memories because of my close relationship with the Ruthenbergs and my enchantment with a place that had rain and grass and where the houses had basements and the countryside offered cherry picking. To my parents, thank you for driving Michael and me some two thousand miles to give us a view of our nation and a summer with our cousins. I'm sorry I was an irritated teenager for most of the road trip.

Thank you so much, Nina Johns, for your critical feedback. Your honesty and competence improved my writing not just for this book but for every other I will ever write. So glad I found you.

And thank you, Judy, for your wisdom. You're a true mentor to me.

My editor Lisa Lee, who read and reread this book—thank you! I feel like God drew us together. Your notes and our conversations made this story shine. And Krissy, you are a gem. Thank you for your help in proofreading and your sweet pep-emails. Dublin soon?

Finally and ever, my husband. My supportive and loving best friend, business partner, and sweetheart: I love you so much. Thank you for *everything*.

Mr. Magoo, always for you.

About the Author

Elizabeth Bromke is the author of the Maplewood series, the Hickory Grove series, and the Birch Harbor series. Each set of stories incorporates family, friends, and love.

Elizabeth lives in the mountains of Arizona, where she enjoys reading, writing, and spending time with her family.

Learn more about the author by visiting elizabethbromke.com today.

Made in the USA
Monee, IL
28 March 2020

24052071R00129